NO BADGE, NO GUN

The Carl Wilcox Mysteries

Available from Walker and Company

NO BADGE, NO GUN

A CARL WILCOX MYSTERY

Harold Adams

WALKER AND COMPANY

New York

First published in the United States of America in 1998 by
Walker Publishing Company, Inc.;
first paperback edition published in 1999.

Published simultaneously in Canada by Fitzhenry and Whiteside,
Markham, Ontario L3R 4T8

Library of Congress Cataloging-in-Publication Data
Adams, Harold, 1923–
No badge, no gun : a Carl Wilcox mystery/Harold Adams.
p. cm.
ISBN 0-8027-3321-2 (hardcover)
I. Title.
PS3551.D367N63   1998
813'.54—dc21   98-26095
CIP
ISBN 0-8027-7575-6 (paperback)

Series design by Mauna Eichner

Printed in Canada
2 4 6 8 10 9 7 5 3 1

To Adrienne, Josh, and Michele,
faithful friends and fans for decades.

NO BADGE, NO GUN

t was hot in Jonesville just before noon as I was finishing up
a window sign and looking forward to getting out of the sun
and into a café, when these two characters came around and
moved close, watching me. The older man, probably in his fifties,
looked aggressive as a football coach. His partner reminded me
of a carnival fighter I'd gone three rounds with in Corden some
years back.

"I hear you're Carl Wilcox," said the older man.

"That's right."

"From Corden."

"Right again, you're doing good."

"I'm Bjorn Bjornson. This is my nephew, Sven. We've heard
stories about you."

"Don't believe everything you hear. How you like this sign?"

"It looks about done," he said, without glancing at it. "If
you're ready for lunch, I'll buy."

"What'll that cost me?"

"You listen to a story. It won't take any longer than eating."

"You've got a deal."

The tough-looking nephew almost smiled.

I cleaned up my brushes, packed my kit, went inside to get paid for the job, and rejoined the men out front. Bjorn steered us directly across the graveled street to Bisel's café and found a booth midway back. We studied the menus, placed our orders, sipped water delivered by the hefty waitress, and looked each other over. Bjorn seemed to be having trouble making up his mind about me. Sven had glanced at him several times after reading the menu but kept his wide mouth shut.

"So, what's the story?" I asked.

Bjorn leaned forward, put his elbows on the table, and frowned.

"Late this spring my niece, Sven's younger sister, was killed in the basement of my church on the south side of town. Some devil raped and strangled her. Nobody's been able to find out who did it, or why she was in the church on a Monday. It wasn't locked. It never has been. She was found the morning after she disappeared. It's plain our local policeman has given up on it. We won't. We can't. I've heard you've solved more than one murder. If you can work on this one, I'll pay for any time lost in your sign painting. If you can solve it, I'll pay you one hundred dollars, cash."

The waitress brought us our orders, and we began eating.

"Tell me about your niece," I said.

"Her name was Gwendolen. She was an honest, bright, and eager girl, a little taller than average, sure of herself, perhaps a little forward. She liked school and most of her teachers, and they liked her. She always got good grades, and more than one teacher told her mother she was smart and a hard worker. A year ago she became the volunteer assistant to the Bible school teacher in our church, and she was so inspired by that teacher, a man from North Dakota, that she told her mother she thought someday she'd marry a missionary and help him convert the heathens in Africa."

"He go back home after the term ended?"

"Yes."

"Know if they kept in touch? Did she write to him, or hear from him?"

"Not that I know of." He glanced at Sven, who shrugged.

"Anybody figure out what time of day she died?" I asked.

"Well, it had to be evening, she'd been home most of Monday. When she went out after supper she didn't say where she was going. Her folks were used to her going out on her own early evenings. In good weather she didn't stay around the house much, and she was such a responsible girl, they didn't always keep track."

"She interested in boys?"

"Of course, she was a normal girl. But there was no special one, or at least none she talked of. The local police officer questioned her classmates. Some said she liked fellows but didn't favor any particular ones. The few boys who admitted talking with her claimed she didn't flirt. Matter of fact, most of them seemed to have the notion she thought they were dumb. That's how it is with young boys, they're put off by girls too smart for them."

That's the way it was for me when I was a kid. I didn't appreciate brains in girls until they blossomed physically, and most of the time found the brighter they were, the more likely they'd snoot me as a roughneck because I fought too often.

"I guess if I'm going to get involved, I'd better talk with the local cop. How do you get on with him?"

Bjornson scowled.

"I don't approve of him. Never have. And he certainly knows I'm not happy with his work on this case—lack of work would be more like it—and he resents the fact I've let everybody know how I feel about it. I'll introduce you and make it plain what I have in mind. He'll probably pretend he's willing to help, but believe me, he won't do anything to make it easy for you. He'll be afraid of getting shown up. Officer Driscoll is a proud man, without the talents that would warrant it."

"Okay, let's go find him."

We didn't find the cop at City Hall or the poolroom but met him on the sidewalk when we turned back toward the café. He was no taller than me, a good bit broader, and some older. His face was red, as if sunburned, but since it was shaded under his broad-brimmed hat I suspected the flush was more from Irish whiskey than old Sol. His nose was broad, his mouth broader, and he had a thick neck, wide shoulders, and a small pot. His uniform was a black suit, a white shirt, and a loosely knotted tie with an open collar. He grinned when the pastor introduced us, and shook my hand with a firm grip.

"I've heard of Carl Wilcox," he said. "The part-time dick and sign painter. What's the pastor trying to put you up to now?"

"I've asked him to look into Gwendolen's murder, since obviously your duties have kept you too busy to work on it."

Driscoll's grin broadened. "The pastor," he told me, "has always been our most concerned citizen in every department. Being a man at God's right hand, he has an awful responsibility, which gets a bit out of bounds where the family's concerned."

Bjornson didn't bother responding. He asked me to come around to the parsonage immediately south of the Lutheran church after I was through with Driscoll, and left us with his nephew in tow.

The cop and I ambled along the wide empty street called Dakota Avenue.

"I hear you served some time," he said.

"Yup. Two years in the army and about the same in stir."

"Which was worse?"

"It was near a toss-up. I suppose the liquor handy when you're off duty in the army beat what you could come by in the big house."

He chuckled. "I like a man who can keep his priorities straight. So, what'd the man of God tell you about his niece's murder?"

I told him.

He said that summed it up. It was a bitch of a case, made no sense at all.

"She wasn't a dumb kid who'd let just anybody lead her into a corner like that church basement. We never got a lead on any kid or guy who'd made a big play for her, and if you can believe other kids, she wasn't one of those starry-eyed simps that swallow a line from a smooth talker. To tell you the God's truth, about the only man I can think of in town who could've got that girl down there would be the pastor himself, and even though I'm not crazy about the old bastard, I just can't picture him doing the job. He's one of them Holy Rollers who's convinced he's so damned important God never takes his eyes off him. He might have talked her to death, but that's the worst. His kind are leery of busting any of the Ten Commandments."

"How about his nephew?"

"Not likely. He's the kind of guy picks his girlfriends to impress the crowd. I doubt he ever noticed his sister till he found her dead in that basement."

"It was the brother that found her? How come?"

"Well, he's doing the janitoring this summer. Went there to clean up. There she was."

"What about the Bible school teacher she helped last summer?"

"Chris Kilbride? There's not much doubt she'd have let him

lead her where he would, but he hasn't been back since he finished teaching that class."

"Know where he was when she died?"

"The pastor checked on that. Claims he was home in Wahpeton, North Dakota. The pastor wouldn't believe Chris would harm a mosquito anyway. Probably right. You could about tell from looking at him, Chris likely never did anything wrong in his life."

I guessed I'd be talking to the pastor about that. Nothing in this world raises more doubts in my mind than apparently perfect young men.

"Who'd Sven report to when he found his sister in the basement?"

"The pastor."

"Who examined the body?"

"Well, the only doc in town is Gwen's dad, Doc Westcott. Naturally he got called in. His family'd been up all night, worried about her not coming home."

"How'd he say she died?"

"He figured somebody did it from behind. The forearm across the windpipe. I called in Doc Severance, from Aquatown, sort of a backup, because you might figure it wasn't easy for the father to do a normal checkup on his own kid. Doc Severance said she also had a dislocated shoulder. Probably the killer twisted her arm around up back, then got his other arm across her neck in front. She must've put up a fight."

The whole picture about gave me the fantods. I thanked him and moved on.

astor Bjornson answered my knock and led me into his study off a small living room, where he parked at a desk and waved me into a straight-backed chair facing him. It was a setup deliberately arranged to make visitors feel like truant kids in the principal's office.

"Well?" he said.

"Who told you where Chris Kilbride was when you tried to call him after the murder?"

He gave me a bitter smile. "So. That's our policeman's tack, is it? No more than I expected. Well, sir, I telephoned Rodney Longquist, the man who sent me young Kilbride when I asked for a Bible school instructor. He told me Chris had gone back to his home in Wahpeton. I learned his parents had been in an auto accident, and he went to take over the farm until something got worked out."

"He give you a number you could call?"

"I didn't ask for one. Why bother him when he already had plenty of trouble?"

"You want to give me Longquist's number?"

He gave me a look that let me know I was out of line, but opened a drawer on the right side of his desk, pulled out an address book, and gave me the number.

"You told me she was good in school—was she the best in her class?"

"Well, just about. There was also Zelda Johnson."

"Were they friends?"

He thought they had been a while back, but not much lately. I asked about Zelda's family. He said her father was Zeke, who owned the grocery store and was a fine member of the Lutheran church. After some more talk, during which he tried to warn me against any leads offered by Officer Driscoll, I thanked him and left.

Johnson's Grocery was doing a moderately brisk business late in the afternoon. I spotted three customers, two with youngsters, and shot some time looking through the apple bin, waiting for the man to be free. He was tall and rangy, with thick and straggly brows only partly hidden by heavy black eyeglass rims. I gave him a nickel for my chosen apple and told him I'd been talking with his minister and would like a few words if he could spare the time.

"It depends on who comes in," he said. "What's on your mind?"

I told him what Bjornson had asked me to do and said, if he would be willing, I'd like a little talk with his daughter in the early evening, to see if she could tell me anything about her former classmate.

He said that should be all right He and his wife would sit in.

"Maybe that's not a great idea. It's likely she'd talk more freely if her folks weren't around."

He gave me a hard look. "You really think our daughter would say anything to a stranger she wouldn't say in front of us?"

I grinned at him. "Think back. How would you have reacted when you were a kid?"

After a second's thought, he suddenly grinned. "Okay. I see your point. But I sure can't guarantee she'll tell you anything. Zelda's not exactly predictable. Come around this evening after supper. I'll cue the wife, and we'll let you talk with my girl in the living room."

From the looks of the house it seemed Zeke was doing okay despite the depression. He met me at the door and introduced me to his wife, who was small, brown-haired, and nicely padded. Her blue eyes took me in with a degree of tolerance I don't get from average Norwegian Lutherans, and it was plain this interview with her daughter had her fullest interest. Neither one of them tried to set rules or limits on my talk with her, and that was appreciated.

Zelda was not the spectacled bookworm I expected. She had freshly marcelled hair, blonder than her mother's, with a face unusually round for such a tender young woman. Despite her lack of height, she seemed very grown-up.

When we were seated in the living room, her on the couch, me on an easy chair across from her, I asked if her parents had told her what I was up to. She said yes, but she didn't see how she could be any help.

"Gwendolen and I weren't close after junior high. Actually, we got to be more like rivals. We didn't fight, we just never did anything together anymore."

"Can you tell me who her best friends were?"

"Well, I don't remember any girls. There were a couple fellows."

"Who?"

"I'd guess she probably liked Bobby Cartwright about as well as anybody. He sat behind her in Miss Stewart's English class, and they traded notes sometimes. He made her laugh."

"Ever see them together outside of school?"

"A few times. Like downtown and in the soda fountain. It wasn't anything real obvious. I mean, she didn't give him goo-goo eyes or anything like that. But you'd see them giggling a lot. And in civics class she sat behind Jimmy Hackett. They didn't whisper in class—nobody did in front of Mr. Norberg. He never missed anything, and everybody was careful because they didn't want to offend him."

"He was a favorite teacher?"

"Oh sure. Nearly all the other teachers are awfully old and treat you like you're a little kid. Mr. Norberg is respectful, and we all wanted to please him."

"He ever talk with kids outside of class?"

"Sometimes in the hall, just outside. I can remember seeing Gwendolen talk to him. She'd come early and be by the door and would ask him a question about things we'd been reading. She was a great one for shining up to teachers."

I asked if she knew what church Mr. Norberg went to. She had no idea.

"Where do you go?"

"Lutheran."

No, she had never seen him there.

"Know any girlfriends of Gwendolen?"

She said she couldn't think of any.

I went back to Pastor Bjornson and asked if Gwendolen's parents would talk to me. He didn't much like the idea but agreed to give it a try and called to make an appointment.

The mother answered. Her name was Martha, and I learned she was Bjorn's sister. She agreed I could come.

Martha looked more like Bjornson's niece than his sister. She seemed half his age and had none of his belligerence, in style or appearance. Her hair was light brown, her eyes deep blue and widely spaced. She greeted Bjornson warmly but looked at me with a combination of sadness and doubt before leading the way into their parlor. She waved us toward a blue-patterned couch and sat, frowning at me rather primly, on a slender chair by an upright piano, resting her left arm on the closed keyboard cover.

"I can't imagine," she said, "what good will come of a new investigation."

"It would at the least make us believe we'd done all we could to find justice," said Bjorn. "We certainly won't ever get it from Officer Driscoll's feeble efforts."

I gathered this was not a new topic of discussion in the family.

Martha nodded abstractedly and asked if we'd like coffee. Before I could say no, Bjorn urged her on; she excused herself and moved into the kitchen. I looked around the room. It was better furnished than average—the carpet was Persian style, if not the real thing, the piano looked freshly varnished, and there were pictures of Roman ruins and Greek statues on the walls. Over the brick fireplace was a family portrait, with the mother between her son and daughter, seated on a couch, and the father standing behind them. Gwendolen's hair was light blond. Her eyes resembled her mother's, but her mouth was wider and hinted at a smile. The parents were soberly formal. Sven looked bored.

"That picture was taken early this spring, not long before Gwendolen's death," Bjorn told me. "It doesn't do her justice."

"Looks good to me."

"She was finer than it shows. Much finer."

I wondered if she had been as much admired while alive.

When Martha returned with a tray of cups and a coffeepot,

I asked if she'd heard Gwendolen speak of the two boys Zelda mentioned. She had not.

"Who were her girlfriends?"

"Becky Simpson and Kate Graff. They were very close all through grade school. I don't remember hearing of or seeing them much in the last couple years. I'm afraid she may have outgrown them."

"What about Zelda?"

"Pretty much the same story—except Zelda lasted a bit longer."

I asked if her daughter had talked much about her civics teacher. He had been mentioned, yes, but obviously hadn't made the deep impression Chris Kilbride did. Or at least, she had not talked about him as much.

"Did she get teased some about the Bible school teacher?"

"Well, I guess so. Certainly Sven kidded her, and I'm sure some classmates did."

"What about her father?"

"He told her in no uncertain terms that she talked about him too much. He's never had any patience with idle chatter like that."

"Where's your husband now?" I asked.

"He's at the Petersons', delivering her baby. They have a farm west of town. I've no idea when he might get home. If you want to talk with him, he could probably see you sometime tomorrow."

"Fine."

I mentioned that another classmate seemed to think Gwendolen might have had a special interest in the civics teacher. Martha smiled.

"Gwendolen had a very special interest in any teacher who taught a course that interested her. She rather cultivated close relationships with people like that. Everything about teaching interested her. She even talked with the principal several times. Asking questions about the problems of running a school."

I got the names of the principal and the civics teacher and the addresses of Gwendolen's former girlfriends, thanked her for her time and patience, and left.

≪ 3 ≫

I n the morning I went over my list of prospects and picked Norberg, the civics teacher, as the first target of the day. Bjorn had told me the teacher lived on the west side of town and spent summer vacations in a cabin on Lake Kampy where he fished, swam, kept a garden, and wrote things he hoped to sell. The pastor didn't know or care what sort of things they might be.

It took a while, but I finally located the cabin in a wooded area at the southern end of the lake. Norberg was fishing off the dock with a long bamboo pole, and wore pale blue, baggy slacks and a white short-sleeved shirt that showed his tanned, almost hairless arms. He glanced back when he felt my presence on the dock, which wasn't the sturdiest I ever walked.

"Any luck?" I asked.

He smiled ruefully and shook his head.

"Haven't caught a half a dozen fish from here in that many years. This is just an excuse to stand admiring the view and day-dreaming. I suppose you're Wilcox."

"How'd you guess?"

"The word's around. A guy my size, with a dimpled chin, black hair, and brown eyes. Asking questions of anyone who knew Gwendolen."

He pulled his line out of the water, clamped the line in, cut the worm off the hook, and laid the pole down on the deck.

"Care for coffee?" he asked.

I said fine, and we left the shuddering dock and walked a narrow dirt path up to the cabin. It had a sagging screened porch with a table and a couple chairs on the right, and a rickety porch swing on rusty chains to the left.

"I inherited this lake mansion from my father about four years ago," he told me. "Sit down here—I've got coffee keeping warm on the burner inside."

He was back in seconds with two white mugs. There was cream and sugar on the table.

"So you're looking into Gwendolen's death? How can I help you?"

"Tell me anything you can about her. How she acted toward other kids, grown-ups in general, you in particular."

"Well, to begin with, she was a born teacher's pet. A dream student. She had a good head, very quick, exceptionally alert. Her one great weakness was—I don't know quite how to describe it, but she was very self-centered and pretty innocent-minded in some ways. I mean, perhaps her judgment wasn't the best. Frankly, she was very flirtatious and had no subtlety. Being smarter than most of your contemporaries can give a youngster a false sense of security. I don't think Gwendolen had any fears. That's refreshing in a young girl, but it can antagonize classmates and get her into trouble."

"Did she flirt with you?"

"Absolutely. Oh, she wasn't terribly obvious, but she loved to play on adult weaknesses. She was always letting me know how terribly knowledgeable I was and how much she could learn from me, even how dependent she was. But mind you, this was all in public places. Ninety-five percent in the high school halls, or in the room with other students present. I remember one time talking with her on the street in front of the soda fountain. But, if this is what you're working around to, we never had a private conference of any length, never so much as shared a table in a café or fountain. As much as I appreciated her flattery, I have never thought I was as brilliant as she kept suggesting, but I am also not dumb enough to permit any relationship with a girl her age that could possibly cause me embarrassment, or harm her reputation."

"She ever ask about your writing?"

He looked sheepish. "Well, yes, in fact."

"What kind do you do?"

"Well, a little poetry, a lot of fiction. Nothing's come of it."

"You show her any of it?"

"No. Never." He managed to laugh. "I'm afraid it's all too self-revealing and amateurish."

"She ever come to your office?"

"Never. I share an office with Miss Warford. It's anything but private. And Gwendolen was not about to try vamping me in that formidable lady's presence."

"Her uncle is positive she'd never be coaxed into a place like the church basement by a stranger. Can you think of anybody she was close enough to that she'd invite them down there?"

"Only the Bible school teacher. From what little I could observe, she was never really interested in any of her classmates that way. She teased a few of the boys along in class, but I don't remember seeing her talking in the halls with one, or walking with any of them around the grounds. She did very few things with other kids."

"How'd you know about the Bible school teacher?"

"Well, several of the kids mentioned him. So did Gwendolen. It was plain she'd chosen him as her mentor."

"You didn't know him?"

"We met at a church social or two."

"What'd you think of him?"

He shrugged. "We didn't really get acquainted. Maybe I was afraid of getting converted. From all I'd heard I half expected to find a halo around his head. He was tall, blond, soft-spoken. Not your Bible-thumping type. I could picture him hypnotizing the ladies with his blue eyes, bright toothy smile, and princely style. Struck me more as a man who might come from Boston instead of Wahpeton."

"You didn't like him?"

He grinned. "I can see you really are a detective. Keen sensitivity. I confess. He had too much going for him. I was most happy when he went away, and I hope he never comes back."

"And you think Gwendolen had a crush on him."

"Probably every girl in town did—from six to sixty and beyond."

"Can you think of any reason at all why she'd go into the basement of that church that night?"

"Who knows? Maybe she was nostalgic about the sessions with Chris Kilbride. That's where their classes were held. Maybe she went down there to commune with his spirit. Who can figure the mind of a fifteen-year-old girl?"

It was plain I couldn't.

« 4 »

I asked Norberg if Miss Warford taught any classes Gwendolen took. He said no, but since she was the school librarian, Gwendolen had seen a good deal of her, and yes, she was in town this summer. I'd find her at the city library next to City Hall. She was filling in for the regular librarian, who'd taken a maternity leave.

At first glance, it was hard to figure why Norberg had called Miss Warford a formidable woman. She looked small sitting behind a desk, working on a stack of cards, when I walked in, and all I saw was dark brown curly hair. She didn't glance up until I stopped in front of her desk. Then her golden brown eyes took me in for a second before she said, "How do you do?"

Each word was distinct, none of your "howjado" stuff.

"As well as I can," I answered, and asked if she could spare a few minutes to talk about Gwendolen.

She pushed the stack of cards to one side and tipped her head toward a chair by the wall beside her.

"Pull it around, Mr. Wilcox."

"Carl," I said, and sat down.

"All right, Carl. I'm Hazel, although around here I've about forgotten it. What do you think you can get from me?"

"Some help. I'm getting mixed messages about Gwendolen, the murdered girl. Like to hear what you thought of her."

"How mixed?"

"Nothing wild. She seems to have been smart, ambitious, not much excited about her classmates, pretty interested in male teachers. How'd she strike a woman like you?"

"Well, I can't claim that a high school girl who only came around to get books she wanted to read bared her soul to me. I know she was a precocious and a heavy reader. When she first asked for *War and Peace*, I suspected it was to impress me—or maybe someone else. She didn't seem terribly disappointed that we didn't have a copy in stock. I couldn't resist offering her my copy, and to my surprise, she took it. The big surprise was, she actually read it."

"You're sure?"

"Positive. We discussed it in detail. She was disappointed that Pierre was the hero through the body of the work. She preferred Prince Andrei, and was much taken by Natasha. Who did you like?"

"Natasha. Can you figure anyone around at the time that Gwendolen would've gone into the church basement with?"

"No. That's a complete mystery to me, as it is to everyone else."

"How do you think she felt about Norberg?"

"I think she preferred summers. Don't wince, I'm only kidding. I think he was too short for her. She much preferred the tall, blond Bible teacher."

"But he was long gone."

"True. We all have to settle for what's available, don't we? No, I'm afraid Harlan Norberg is a most unlikely suspect. A church basement is the last place he'd think of for romancing, even if he were so inclined, and I don't believe he is. I suspect Harlan's a bit of a coward with women."

I wasn't sure I wanted to push that line, so I tried switching her to another.

"Did you ever see Gwendolen talking with classmates in the library?"

"Classmates don't talk to each other in my library. If they want conversation, they go somewhere else."

"She ever come around regularly with anyone?"

"Not regularly. I saw her come and go with Jimmy Hackett a time or two. She sort of treated him like a younger brother."

"Did you know the Bible teacher at all?"

"Not well. I'm not much interested in Bible blonds, to tell you the truth. Maybe it's a snobbish thing. They just don't appeal to me."

"You got any plans for supper?"

"No."

"How about we have it together?"

She smiled. "You have that many more questions to ask about Gwendolen?"

"Probably not. But I might sneak in a couple about other citizens. Like the pastor and his nephew."

She laughed. "Okay, why not? I'd invite you to my place, but I'm not that well set up for cooking and wouldn't want to start a rumor wave anyway."

"I don't think you give a damn about rumors."

She laughed again. "You're wrong. I love them. I'm through here at five. You want to pick me up at six?"

She gave me the address and kiddingly offered to draw a map, but I said I could manage without.

She roomed in Abigail Smith's house, which was in the middle of the block on a quiet side street. Abigail was an old maid, an only child who'd nursed her aging mother through some twenty years of senility and was awarded the house and inheritance enough to scrape by on. She was sitting on the porch with a *Reader's Digest* in her lap when I approached, and gave me a critical going-over with disapproving eyes. I said good evening, and before she could respond, Hazel appeared and introduced us. She gave me the details of Abigail's past as we walked toward the restaurant.

"I can see why you didn't want to eat at home," I said.

"Oh, Abigail's not so bad when you get to know her. But she's not comfortable with men. And she won't let me into her kitchen except to eat. In the beginning I offered to do dishes, but she won't let me touch them once we finish eating. It's not a bad deal for me."

She had nothing more to give me about Gwendolen and was a little hesitant about discussing the pastor.

"I don't really know him that well. I've attended his church a few times—he's an intelligent speaker who tries to persuade his audience, rather than bully or harangue them. You get a feeling there's a man up there with very deep convictions, who hasn't let them get out of hand in his human relationships. I haven't been exposed to many like him. He seems actually capable of understanding that reasonable people might not accept everything he has to offer. Not many dedicated preachers I've met can do that."

None I had could.

"You ever hear how he got along with the Bible school guy?"

"No. I mean, it's a subject that never came up in any of the company I keep."

"Gwendolen ever say anything to you about her uncle?"

"Never. The only man she ever spoke to me about was Chris

Kilbride, the Bible man. I think he probably had much to do with her reading habits and directions."

By the time we were halfway through our meal she had taken over the questioning and was digging into me. She wanted to know how the devil I had got myself into prison.

"It was easy. One, I never had any money but got involved with a couple women who needed it. Two, the only time bright ideas came on how to get cash quick was when I'd been having more than enough booze and wasn't exactly at my sharpest."

"Tell me about it."

"Well, the first time I went gaga over a young widow I met after leaving home, when I was seventeen and bumming around in Minneapolis. I got a temporary job delivering groceries and met this young woman with a baby who was having a tough time and needed money to pay the rent. She wasn't much older than me and sweeter than a box of Fanny Farmer candy. When I was let off the job I'd been working on, I got down a bit and managed to bum enough money for a few drinks, they set me up with ambition to try knocking over a jewelry store to help the widow. A guy I drank with loaned me a .32, and I went into this jewelry store downtown near quitting time. Waited till it was empty and went in with the gun, which wasn't loaded because I didn't figure on shooting it. The minute I put the gun on the owner, an older couple wandered in. I got them herded over near the counter by the cash register and told them to lay down. The guy went down like a rabbit, but the lady was wearing a white dress and just wouldn't do it. So I let her put her hands up, and of course just then a cop wandered by outside, spotted her, and charged in. For some reason he didn't believe me when I said it was all just a joke, not even when he found my gun was empty. So I went to jail. The next day I was up before the judge and pleaded guilty, and probably would have got off easy, but he asked me if I wished to express my regrets and I said yes, I was blamed sorry I hadn't made the lady get down on the floor so the cop wouldn't have seen her. The judge didn't think that was funny, and I got a year."

"Tell me more," she said.

"In the second case, a few years later, I was working for this Montana widow who owned a ranch and claimed she couldn't afford enough cattle to make ends meet. She got pretty cozy with me—it wasn't hard, since she was about as shy as a tarantula and sexy as Garbo. One night we had a few drinks, and she told about this herd of cattle owned by a neighbor rancher who let his stock roam near her territory, and she got across the notion that we could sort of borrow them and make some brand changes. With the combination of booze and her bed style of persuasion, it all made fine sense at the time. Actually it might have worked out okay, but my mare stepped in a gopher hole and broke her leg, which slowed me down enough to let the rancher's boys nail me on their range. So I got another stretch, this time in Stillwater."

"And you didn't say anything dumb to the sentencing judge, huh?"

"Came near. Almost said I was sorry my horse got a broken leg. But I stifled it."

"So how'd you manage to get away from a career in crime?"

"Well, having flunked my first two courses, I just went back home and worked in my old man's hotel. Then I met this painter guy, we hit it off, and he taught me the tricks of the trade. Best thing ever happened to me. I was never as good as he was, but he was a hell of a teacher, and I could get by. Gave me a chance to roam around, paying my way, meeting folks."

"How'd you get into detecting?"

"Fell in. Being an ex-con, I was a suspect in anything that went wrong wherever I went for a few years, and I started figuring out who done it a couple times when it kept me from getting stuck, and then one day Corden needed a temporary cop the worst way, and as somebody said, they got the worst kind. That sort of set up my bona fides, and I've been milking it ever since."

"Don't you want to settle down someday?"

"Not really. Never saw any big advantages in it."

"You know what I think?"

"Nope."

"I think you're playing a role. You think it's romantic. Like being the stranger in town, the man talked about, the drifting lover, all the joys without responsibilities or commitments."

"Sounds good."

"Don't you ever get lonely?"

"Yeah. And I get tired, and hungry, thirsty, and too hot or cold. They're all temporary. So far."

"And one day you'll get old."

"Not in one day."

She smiled, drank some coffee, and leaned against the booth back.

"I'll admit," she said, "I envy you. One can get very tired of responsibilities, the business of being dependable, predictable, and dull."

"I guess you'd have to work pretty hard at that."

"Full-time. So how are you doing in the suspect department?"

"No progress. What do you do for excitement?"

"Just about nothing. I don't go to the local dance hall, once in a while take in a movie at the local theater—alone. Listen to my radio some but turn it off early so's not to offend Abigail, who's an early retirer."

"No guys?"

"Harlan Norberg came the closest. I'm not quite sure what his problem is, but I suspect he's only interested in the sure thing and didn't think I'd qualify. As far as the townies go, they're mostly just interested in local girls, ones they went through school with. A woman from the outside is too alien, so I've had no serious approaches from any of them."

After finishing dinner, we walked up by the school. It was on a gentle rise, a dark brown building that looked older than it could actually be in this territory. She told me she enjoyed teaching grade schoolers, had no serious trouble with keeping discipline, and generally liked the kids.

"They're manageable up until you get to seventh- and eighth-graders. I'd rather be a dishwasher in a hash house than teach junior high."

"So you live with books."

"I'm afraid so."

"Care to take in the dance this coming Saturday night?"

She smiled. "Yes, I'd like that. I won't even mind if you drop around to ask more questions before then. Good night."

And she was gone inside. Not even a handshake.

5

r. Westcott's nurse told me he was too busy to see me when I went to his office in the morning. She said he was booked solid for the day and seemed very pleased about it.

"Ask if he'll have lunch with me."

"He's already engaged."

"He's not engaged, lady, he's married. And he's the father of a girl who got murdered, and I'm trying to find out who did it, and it seems like he just might be interested in helping me get this job done. If he's not, it raises some interesting questions. You follow me?"

That brought what they call a pregnant silence. Then she suggested I sit down and wait until the doctor finished with his present patient.

"No, thanks. I'll be moving around, but I'll come back. I'm not asking for a couple hours, just a few minutes. If you can squeeze me in later, it could avoid some embarrassment."

She said she was sure he would work me in and managed to make it sound respectful.

It was lots less trouble getting at Bobby Cartwright. He

worked at the grocery store and was candling eggs in the back room when I went around. Made me think of the days I'd done that job for my old man when he helped run a cousin's grocery in Michigan. My older cousin worked there too and used to come around and bump my elbow so I'd jam the egg into the light frame and break it, and have the mess to clean up.

Bobby was about my height, not quite skinny, with dark hair combed tight to his round skull, and innocent blue eyes. He was happy to knock off a few minutes and answer questions. Said he'd never been close enough to Gwendolen that she told him anything about people close to her.

"You know her dad, Doc Westcott?"

"Sure. He took out my tonsils and adenoids when I was seven."

"How'd you like him?"

"Well, I guess he's okay. We didn't, you know, get chummy there at the hospital. I kinda got this feeling he was a guy who'd cut out your liver if you gave him any trouble."

"Why'd you think that?"

"Well, it was the way he told my parents what to do when I was going home. He was real bossy. The nurses about jumped out of their skins when he told them to do anything."

"Gwendolen ever talk about him?"

"Oh yah. She always let us know he was the town doctor and smarter than anybody else around."

"Think she liked him?"

"Well, she sure liked to brag about him."

"I guess you weren't real crazy about her."

He frowned, uncomfortably, and looked toward the front of the store.

"Actually, I kind of liked her, but it was tough, because she was so smart and talked about books I hadn't read and other stuff. Other times she'd be real fun. It sort of mixed me up."

"Ever kiss her?"

The idea seemed to shock him. "Oh gosh, no. She wasn't that kind of girl."

"Know any fellas at school she went for?"

"None of the students, no."

"But she went for some of the teachers?"

"Well, I guess you could say that. She had a crush on the Bible school guy, and thought Mr. Norberg was real neat. She liked Miz Warford real well. Some kids thought she was just shining up to all of her teachers for good grades, but she was too smart to have to do that. I think she really liked just hanging around and talking with them a lot. She said they were smart and understanding and appreciated her."

I couldn't get to Jimmy Hackett easily; he lived and worked on his parents' farm west of town. I got the location down and decided to wait until he was through working and home in the evening for dinner and sleep.

My second call at Doc Westcott's office got me in to see him toot sweet.

He was sitting slumped behind his desk and looked drained as an enema victim. At the sight of me, he straightened up but didn't stand. His eyes, behind heavy bifocals, took me in with something between annoyance and resignation.

"So," he said.

I glanced at his examining table by the wall and moved into the straight-backed chair facing his desk.

"How do you get along with Pastor Bjornson?" I asked.

"What's that got to do with anything?" he asked, scowling.

"I just wonder if you resent him hiring me to poke into this problem."

He took off his glasses, rubbed his eyes gently, and placed the glasses on the low desk. The scowl turned to a thoughtful frown. "I suppose, in a way, I do. This—loss—is something I've had trouble dealing with. Somehow I can't get caught up in the wild pursuit of retribution, revenge, or even justice. I can't even think in that line. I only want her back. I don't want to think why it was done, or how, or who. Does that seem unnatural to you?"

I shook my head.

"Really? You're not just humoring me?"

"No."

He looked down at his hands, then back at me again. "I keep thinking of how little I knew her, actually. How little I understood. She was a very, very bright girl. I found myself resenting how quickly she was growing up, how little she seemed to care about my opinions or advice. A man expects his daughter to be dependent. Gwendolen wasn't that kind. The weird thing is that now I remember, I had the same attitude toward my father, and how surprised I was, when I reached maturity, to discover he was actually a very intelligent and understanding man. Gwendolen will never come to that—"

He broke off, got to his feet, and walked to the window overlooking a small, sun-scorched lawn. After a moment he came back, sat down, and managed to smile at me.

"What can I tell you that might be helpful?"

As it turned out, not much. He hadn't known her friends; he was well informed only about her good grades and her close relationship with several of her more talented teachers, and felt quite content with the relationship between his daughter and her mother. He admitted to some small annoyance when he felt Gwendolen became condescending toward her mother, but he said that was a rare occurrence. He claimed he had merely been amused by her absorption in the Bible school teacher and what he called her brief fascination with the idea of doing missionary work.

"You're saying that was just a phase, that she got over it?"

"Oh, yes. She got hold of Thomas Paine's *Age of Reason* and became, at once, an agnostic. That was about a month after the holy man left us."

A patient showed up a few moments later, and figuring I'd picked up all I was going to get, I thanked the doctor and left.

❦ 6 ❧

fter supper alone, I drifted around to the pool hall. It was run by a skinny scarecrow named Epcott who had no objection to my shooting a few rounds on my own while no one else was around. He asked how the detecting racket compared with painting signs when it came to paydays. I said it was sign painting by a mile.

"So how come you're sticking your neck out?"

I knocked a four ball into a corner pocket and straightened up for a closer look at the man.

"You think I got a problem here?"

"We already got a cop."

"He didn't seem bothered when we talked the business over."

"Well then, you got no problem—maybe."

I leaned my rump on the pool table edge and chalked my cue tip.

"You mind telling me a little bit about this cop? How long's he been on the job?"

"About five years. Driscoll's from Sioux Falls. Brought in by our mayor in those days, old man Burke. Seems like they knew each other somewhere, the army, I think. Met somewheres in France during the big war."

"You like him?"

"Burke was a good man," he said, and lit a fresh cigarette from the butt of his earlier smoke.

"I meant Driscoll."

"Well now, he must be a good cop. Except for the Gwendolen thing, we ain't had no crime in town to mention since he took over."

"There was a lot before him?"

He grinned. "Not that I remember."

Two locals came in, ending our discussion. Eventually more guys drifted around, and I played three games and won the last two. The betting was so low it just paid for my games and a bag of tobacco.

I thought briefly of going to Jimmy Hackett's home for some talk, but decided I'd rather catch him alone than in the family circle and put it off.

By eleven I decided to sack out and drove my Model T to the north side of town where farmer Sandstrom had earlier agreed to let me camp at the edge of his windbreak if my campfire was kept small and under control. In exchange I painted his name on his mailbox, which pleased him fine and tickled his wife, Mia, enough to make her come around and offer me breakfast the next morning. She was a heavyset woman with small, bright blue eyes and a smile that dimpled her round cheeks and showed clean, gapped teeth.

She wanted to know all about my experiences as a traveling sign painter, and before long it was plain she'd heard stories about me unrelated to painting and was eager to pump me about murder in South Dakota.

She hit me in about my third-weakest spot. I was still talking by ten o'clock, and had eaten three eggs, four slices of toast, and a rasher of bacon while swilling down enough coffee to float a goose.

In the midst of all this, I worked some at getting a little information from her. It was plain Mia worked hard at keeping track of city gossip, but living on the edge of town made it hard for her to pick up much that was reliable. She went to church and had friends, though, so I got a little help.

Yes, she'd heard about the awful murder of Gwendolen. At first it sounded as though the victim had been something of a bright saint, but then it became evident there had been reports of her boldness with teachers and her generally superior attitude toward classmates. There were faint rumors involving doubts about her virtue, but since she was so young, these were only hinted at.

When I finally left, Mia invited me back for dinner, saying her husband would love to hear my stories. I thanked her but made no promises, explaining that things could get complicated when a man is messing with a murder investigation.

Her eyes glowed with excitement.

In town I went around to the schoolhouse and found the principal, Mr. Hanson, who said he taught history in addition to his loftier duties and assured me Gwendolen had been an ideal student, who not only scored high in tests but asked intelligent questions in class. No, he hadn't noticed that she showed any particular interest in any of her classmates, male or female, and she had not made any overt effort to charm him personally.

I wasn't certain whether his comments were defensive or not. He didn't strike me as a man with enough imagination to guess anyone would ever suspect him of the slightest indiscretion. He confessed that generally he found girls inept in his courses and had a theory that they were generally better off when they concentrated on wifely pursuits and harmless things like poetry and grammar.

After a solitary lunch at the restaurant, I went back to visit Bjornson and told him about my day so far. He took it all in soberly, then said he'd heard from a friend that the town cop was making inquiries into my past and had confirmed I had a prison record. Since that hadn't been a secret anywhere I remembered visiting, this seemed like a waste of the cop's time, and I asked if Bjornson hadn't already known it.

"With people like you, there are so many stories, a man can't tell which to believe. It rather comes down to the fact that no one questions your talent for solving murders, and responsible law enforcement people have seen fit to cooperate with you. That's enough for me. I tell you what Officer Driscoll has been up to so that you won't forget he's not going to help in any way and will more than likely attempt to interfere. Be careful."

I spent the rest of the afternoon looking up Gwendolen's two grade school friends, Becky Simpson and Kate Graff. Neither one of them gave me any help, just talked of what an awful thing her death was and how she'd be missed. Neither one of them seemed to know much about how Gwendolen felt about anyone in her life beyond the Bible school teacher. Both seemed uncomfortable about that relationship. It wasn't obvious, just something I sensed because of their reluctance to comment about him beyond parroting the reports I'd heard of his talents as a teacher.

Late in the afternoon I telephoned Hazel and asked if she'd like to have dinner with me. She said that was a splendid idea, how about picking her up at six?

She wore a dress that was mostly white and fit her a bit too modestly. No doubt she dressed for the school board, not young men. Since Abigail's house was only two blocks from downtown, I had walked to make the pickup, and we strolled along the still-hot sidewalk under cottonwoods, elms, and box elders before reaching the barren area of downtown. We got a table by the wall, where we attracted more attention than my partner welcomed. She frowned irritably as we examined menus and discussed the choices. She told me the chicken dinner was probably the best the place had to offer, we both ordered it, and suddenly she lightened up and even smiled.

"From what I've heard of you," she said, "inviting a woman to a restaurant seems rather out of character. Even inviting me to the dance seems a bit formal for you."

"It seems to me South Dakotans are pretty hard up for things to talk about if I get as much attention as you say. You sure you aren't just figuring out lines on your own?"

She laughed, tilting her head back some, put her elbows on the table and her chin in her hands. "Don't you like being analyzed?"

"Any attention I get from a good-looking woman is appreciated. Why do you think Harlan Norberg calls you formidable?"

"Because he's a vulnerable man. Oversensitive, very low self-confidence. Which is a shame, actually, because he's intelligent and understanding in most ways. People who want to be artists, poets, or writers of any kind and haven't managed to sell or publish anything get terribly thin-skinned. He senses that I have self-confidence and few doubts—he probably thinks I don't have any doubts at all, which certainly isn't the case, but I don't expose them. In his eyes, I'm a strong woman, and while he respects that, it also antagonizes him. Fortunately he's a man who can generally disguise or hide his antagonism. He let you see how he felt, I'll bet, very deliberately. Warning you, and at the same time showing you he was one of the boys."

"That's about the way I figured it," I admitted.

"How come you don't work in a city like Sioux Falls, or even Minneapolis?"

"Too many people. In small towns you can get away from it all by walking a few blocks. I like getting to know a place in a day or two. Who runs it, why, all that. It's easy to get acquainted."

"If you like getting acquainted, how come you're always moving?"

"To get acquainted with more people."

"Couldn't you do that quicker in a big city?"

"I'm not in any hurry. Besides, city people aren't as acquaintable. Why're you working in a small town?"

"Because it was easy to find a job, living costs are low, and I can walk to work."

When we were through eating and I'd paid the bill, we went out to stroll the town a bit and wandered to a small, barren park where there were a couple softball diamonds. A few kids were playing a pickup game, and we watched a few moments. One kid, probably no more than thirteen, belted the ball like a pro. Made me think of my older nephew.

"Did you play ball as a kid?" she asked.

"Some. Just sandlot stuff."

"Never on a team?"

"No."

"Always the loner. I was like that. Played tennis, even golf a little. I guess you never got into that sort of thing either."

"Never."

"Ice skating, skis?"

"Couldn't afford the gear."

"Sad."

"I didn't suffer any."

She was silent for a while and then suggested we walk some

more. We headed west, which took us up a gradual slope to a low hilltop overlooking much of the town.

"I think," she said, blinking against the lowering sun, "this will be my last summer in Jonesville. Somehow I have to find greater possibilities than this offers."

"In jobs or men?"

She glanced at me and grinned. "Both."

"How'd you get along with your folks?"

"What makes you ask that?"

"Nosiness. Pure and simple."

She faced me, tilted her head a bit, and folded her arms, smiling.

"Did you have trouble with your father?"

"He thinks he had trouble with me."

"From what I've heard, that's not hard to figure. You sound like a parent's nightmare. All right, I suppose I was a problem too. But I never reacted as strongly as you obviously did. My father was a born first sergeant. All male. Down deep I think he hated women. He didn't understand anything about them and didn't want to. My mother, luckily, had a great sense of humor, but she was smart enough to know better than let it show around him. At least most of the time. She never bucked him directly. In my early teens I thought that was hypocritical, even sneaky. She died when I was only seventeen. In childbirth. I think he let it happen because he couldn't believe the baby was his. He never said as much, but I sensed it. I was off to college then, at North Dakota University. They were living on a farm near Minot. That's getting up near the Canadian border, so you can imagine how remote it might have been. Before that, my father had been a high school teacher and football coach in Grand Forks. He quit at the end of the season and took over the claim his father had taken way back. There's no question in my mind that he'd left the farm as a teenager because he hated that life, and he went back because he was positive mother was pregnant by another man. He took her there to punish her for her adultery, and maybe even made certain she wouldn't survive giving birth. There was no doctor around—no one examined her or the baby, which he claimed was stillborn. The local minister came, accepted his story, and made the funeral arrangements."

Her emotions choked off anything further; she stopped talking and began walking. I stayed close.

"What'd he do after that?"

She swallowed a couple times before answering. "Moved to Minot and taught history and coached the football team. I heard the team did quite well." She glanced at me. "I never saw him again. He died in a car accident when I was twenty-one."

Her story was enough to make me think my old man, Elihu, had been too good for me.

She told me a little about her life in school. She'd gone with several fellows there but never got much involved. They either reminded her of her father or seemed too lightweight.

"Actually," she said, with a grimace, "I was probably an awful stick. Moody, too involved with reading about life to live it for myself. Nearly all of the professors who amounted to much were men, and they made me think of my father. I thought several of the female profs were fine, I suppose because so many were single, and independent of men."

Eventually we drifted back down into town and checked the dance hall. The band was already playing, and we saw young girls dancing with each other. Hazel told me the manager let them in free until the regular crowd began to appear, then shooed them out.

It was a surprise to find she was a great dancer. From our talk it seemed likely she'd be one of those women who want to lead, or simply aren't interested enough to pay attention to the beat. On slow numbers we danced close, and she allowed more contact than most women I've known would so early. After a little while a couple guys came around during breaks to ask for dances with her, and she accepted. I watched and saw she didn't let them get as close, which made me feel pretty good. I didn't ask anybody else for a round. Mostly they seemed too young or involved with each other.

After Hazel returned from her second partner, we shared another set, and she told me the guy she'd just been with had some interesting news.

"Chris Kilbride's in town—you remember? The Bible school teacher."

"Where's he staying?"

"I imagine at the widow Page's place. That's where he stayed when he was teaching Bible school last year, and she hasn't had another boarder I know of."

We went to the beer parlor and had a glass apiece, talked some, and then she said that was all for her, so I asked would she lead me by the widow's house and show me where Kilbride might be. She did, and the house was dark.

"Want to go in and roust him out?" she asked.

"I'll try him tomorrow. You willing to go for a ride?"

"No. You got as close to me on the dance floor as you're going to tonight, so don't make any plans."

"The way it went in the dance hall kind of got my hopes up."

"Yes, I could tell. It was pretty flattering in a way, but I suspect any woman has that effect on you. I'm not a first-nighter, Carl. Okay?"

"Sure."

So we walked back to Abigail's place, where she gave me a firm kiss good night and went in.

I walked back to my car, drove to the farm, and sacked out.

✂ 7 ✄

ince it was Sunday the next morning, Officer Driscoll wouldn't be in his office at City Hall. I couldn't be sure which church he'd go to, so I snoozed late and enjoyed a breakfast of bacon, scrambled eggs, and toast with coffee cooked on my grill over a small fire in the shade of an elm tree a few yards from the road.

The restaurant was open for the after-church crowd, and I swung around and found the cop alone at a table near the back. He greeted me with his broad grin and said he bet I'd never guess who he was going to go chat with when he finished his meal.

"Chris Kilbride?"

He looked startled, then laughed. "Well, at least you made it a question. How the hell'd you figure that out?"

"I heard at the dance last night that he was in town. Did you invite him back?"

He shook his head as if in wonder. "You figured that out too, eh? Maybe you're smart as some claim. You also figure I was goosed into it by the good pastor's hiring you, right?"

"It figures."

He leaned back and grinned at me.

"I don't think it's gonna do a damn bit of good, but we gotta go through the motions, right?" He didn't expect a response to that, and I made none. "You ever have a case you couldn't crack?" he asked.

"There were a couple I never got really pinned down, even when I thought I had it figured."

"I'll believe that. You got any notions on this one yet?"

"If the Bible teacher'd still been living in town when it happened, he'd be my first choice, but as it is, it just doesn't seem likely."

He shook his head. "I told you, this one's a bitch. If I could just figure out a way to prove a kid like that could rape and strangle herself, it'd save a hell of a lot of sweat. But I got a feeling that'll never sell. It's about got to be some kid from school, is all I can figure. The hell of dealing with kids is, you almost never got a record to work on. At least not in a town like this."

The wind was up as we walked toward the widow Page's place after finishing and paying our bills in the restaurant.

When Driscoll knocked, the widow came to the door and told us Kilbride was out in back. We walked around and found him staring at tiger lilies growing beside the small outhouse. He had a cup in his hand and was sipping from it when he heard us, lowered it, and looked around.

All the talk I'd heard made me expect he'd be over six feet tall, almost Greek god–like. In fact he looked pale, slender, only averagely taller than me, and vulnerable.

"Officer Driscoll," he said, but he looked at me.

"This," said Driscoll, tipping his head my way, "is Carl Wilcox. He's been hired by Pastor Bjornson to help on this thing, since the man of God hasn't got much faith in me."

Kilbride's pale blue gaze, which took in nothing but my eyes, gave me the notion he thought he could read my soul, or at least wanted to make me think he could. He suddenly looked taller and less vulnerable.

"Are you an old acquaintance of the reverend?" he asked.

"Never met him before this week."

"How'd he happen to hire you?"

"Wilcox," said Driscoll, "has a reputation for pinning killers. He's been on all sides of the law—Pastor Bjornson seems to figure that gives him an edge."

"Really? Would you mind telling me a little about yourself, Mr. Wilcox?"

"Call me Carl. I've no badge nor gun, no club or cuffs. Right now I'm not the question. How about we stick with Gwendolen?"

My shot at cutting him down to size didn't faze him. He smiled and seemed to mean it. "Yes, of course. Do you want to talk out here?" he asked Driscoll. "Or would you be more comfortable inside?"

"Let's use the kitchen. I've heard the widow's coffee is good."

Kilbride nodded, and led the way. The widow produced cups, saucers, cream, and sugar and poured coffee. Then she was gone.

Driscoll creamed and sugared his brew, stirred it briskly, put down his spoon, and after a sip, rested his elbows on the table.

"I didn't tell Wilcox about the anonymous note you got on Gwen. Want to give us the details on that?"

"Of course. And please, let's call her Gwendolen. She hated being called Gwen. If you don't mind?"

Driscoll's scowl said he did, but he nodded in agreement.

"The note came in the mail about a week after the murder. No return address, and no signature. At the time I was so buried in family problems, it barely made any impression. My father had died two weeks before, and my mother was still suffering from damages caused by their auto accident. I simply couldn't deal with the tragedy in Jonesville too. Now that my mother is recovering quite well and I've been able to get help on the farm to keep things going, I wanted to be here. As you know, Gwendolen was a priceless assistant and a wonderful child—I've never had a better disciple, one with such promise. Frankly, I can't imagine how I can be of any help, but I'm willing, eager, to help you in any way possible."

"You got the note with you?"

"Yes." He reached into his shirt pocket, pulled out a folded tablet sheet, and handed it over.

It was done in ink with bold capital letters: YOUR FAVORITE GWENDOLEN HAS BEEN RAPED AND MURDERED. WHERE WAS YOUR LOVING GOD WHEN THIS WAS DONE?

We stared at the message. Driscoll asked if there was anything in the printing or the wording that gave him a hint who might have sent it.

He shook his head. "All I'm sure of is, whoever wrote it wanted to hurt me, and the good Lord knows he succeeded."

"You got no idea who sent it?" asked Driscoll.

He shook his head sorrowfully.

"I assumed at first that it was someone in my Bible school class. I'm sorry to say, several girls in it were jealous of her because she was so obviously their superior, and she wasn't very good at concealing her awareness of the fact. But the printing is so bold, the message so blunt, I can't quite imagine any of them doing it."

"You know she said something to her parents about wanting to be the wife of a missionary?" I asked.

He reddened some. "Yes, she told me that too."

"And I suppose you'd mentioned along the way that missionary work was your line?"

"It was no secret. And when she mentioned her ambition, I

told her it was most laudable and that I hoped she would find someone her age who would make it possible."

"How'd she take that?"

He looked sheepish. "She gave me a wise smile and said nothing."

"How about boys in your class?" said Driscoll. "Any of them give her a rush?"

"No." The smile changed to a thoughtful frown. "No, you have to remember, she was more mature and taller than any of them. She intimidated the brighter ones and offended those who were put off by her aggessiveness at times."

"You notice any boys who really had it in for her?" I asked.

"I can't believe any of them built up a grudge, or felt the kind of antagonism that would lead to murder and worse. In my experience boys of that age, twelve to fifteen, generally dismiss girls they don't like."

"Did she ever talk to you about her father, or her uncle?"

"I'm sure she wanted very much to impress her uncle. More than once she revealed a deep respect for him. I had the impression she was disappointed that he didn't pay her more attention. It wasn't anything obvious—it's just something I sensed."

"You think she wanted you to believe she considered him special because he was a preacher, and figured that'd make her more attractive to you?"

He smiled, the warmest yet. "That's good. I never thought about it at the time, but it's very possible she thought like that. She was a clever, very thoughtful girl. I wouldn't put it past her."

We went on asking questions. Did she talk of other teachers in any way that would, considering what had happened, make one of them develop ideas that she was encouraging him?

He told us that to the best of his knowledge, the only males important to her were her father, her uncle, and the English teacher, Norberg.

"It is unthinkable that any one of them could have harmed her."

"It had to be somebody she trusted, or she wouldn't have gone down into that church basement with him—or her."

"Well, if she was raped, it could hardly have been a woman."

Since I wasn't sure what proof either Driscoll or the doc had that she'd been raped, I let that ride.

"Can you think of any reason why she'd invite some guy into the church basement?" I asked. "It wasn't a rainy night, or cold, and it doesn't seem like the most romantic setting around."

"Well, it obviously offered privacy that night. I can't think of any other reason. Any more than I can imagine why she'd be tempted to go there if invited, even by someone she was strongly attracted to."

I asked him how well he knew Sven Westcott, the pastor's nephew.

"Not well, why?"

"Did Gwendolen ever talk about him?"

"Not that I can recall. They're not at all alike, from what little I know. Of course, he has been working as janitor for the church—does that give you ideas?"

"Nothing special. Just trying to figure out the whole family. Never know what'll help."

"Well," said Driscoll, "I hope you understand why I got to ask this, but where were you the night Gwen—I mean Gwendolen—got murdered?"

"Home in Wahpeton. There'll be no problem proving that."

"Good, I never doubted you could. When you want, gimme the names of folks who'd know, okay? How long you expect to stay in town?"

"A few days. You want a written list, with addresses?"

"That'd be fine. You gonna visit with Pastor Bjornson?"

"I feel I should, don't you?"

"Oh yeah, I'd say so. Well, thanks for your time, and give our thanks to the widow for the coffee."

We walked through the house without seeing the landlady, and on the front porch Kilbride suddenly asked if we'd heard anything about Gwendolen's having lost her faith before she was murdered. That was news to Driscoll, but I admitted I had heard as much.

"Would you mind telling me about it?"

I said no, why not? Driscoll excused himself and went off, and I told the missionary what the doctor had told me about Gwendolen's rejection of the church after reading Tom Paine. For the first time since we had met, he looked vulnerable, even hurt.

"How awful," he said softly. "So she died without faith."

He looked at me.

"That's the one comfort I had, my conviction that she died saved. Her father told you this? What did he think of it?"

"I doubt he gave it a lot of thought. He just mentioned it, sort of in passing."

"Yes, I suppose he would. He only believes in medicines and surgical tools."

He shook his head, then straightened up slightly and frowned.

"I'll have to talk with him. I'd like to know how Gwendolen happened on Paine. What an appropriate name, incidentally. Well—"

He turned and went back into the house.

I got directions to the Hackett farm from Driscoll and drove out fairly late Sunday afternoon. The wind was whistling across the prairie and whipped away the dust raised by my Model T as it rattled along the graveled road.

The farmhouse stood on a gentle slope facing south, and instead of the usual windbreak of elms, there were scrubby crab apple trees in a thin row out back. A steady west wind herded tumbleweeds across the dusty front yard. You could look in every direction and see only flat prairie with nothing taller than telephone poles along the nearest highway, and fence posts around pastures in the near distance. I parked beside a weary four-door 1930 Chevy and got out. A tall man in a white open-collared shirt appeared behind the screen door in front, pushed it open, and said, "Hi."

He had a face so short of flesh it showed almost every bone surface of his skull. Thin lips barely covered his long teeth, and his nose was a narrow beak.

"Mr. Hackett?" I asked.

"That's right."

"I'm Carl Wilcox. Pastor Bjornson's asked for my help on the Gwendolen Westcott case, and I'm trying to talk with all the classmates that knew her enough to give me a better notion of what she was like."

He took that in with a blank expression, nodded, and said, "Come on in."

Hackett's farmhouse, like most I ever visited, was entered through a side door. Your average farmer only used the front entrance for weddings and funerals, if that. Some had them closed year round. The living room floor was covered by the biggest rag rug I ever saw. It was blamed near wall-to-wall, and if it was missing any color in the rainbow, it wasn't for lack of trying. The furniture was spare and worn, no overstuffed chairs or davenport, no sign of a radio. The pictures were religious scenes, cheap and almost colorless. A small side table supported a battered lamp, centered on a neatly knitted cloth with long tassels.

Hackett waved me toward a wooden rocker beside the wooden-armed couch as his wife appeared in the dining room doorway. She was a tall, thin woman with a pale complexion, large blue eyes, a soft mouth, and a firm chin. Hackett told me her name was Louise but didn't give her my name. It was evident they'd been expecting me. She said she'd get Jimmy.

"If you don't mind," I told Hackett, "I'd like to talk with the boy alone. It'll make things easier for him if he's not worried what you're thinking about his answers to some of my questions."

His long, bony face went from cool to something like frigid.

"What kind of questions you going to ask?"

"Any that'll help me get a clearer picture of what the girl was like. Whether she was likely to have led boys on, or been in love with one of her teachers. So far there's been no way to figure out how she'd wind up in that church basement with somebody who could kill her and do the rest. I think people Officer Driscoll and

I've talked with have been holding out. There's got to be some explanation for how it could happen."

"There's no way Jimmy would've done that thing. He was nothing but a classmate, how'd he know anything?"

"Maybe he doesn't. Don't worry, I'm not suspecting your boy or any of the other kids in the class actually killed her. It seems most likely some adult she trusted did it, but nobody's been able to give us a hint about who that'd be, and I'm hoping a classmate who's smart enough to pay attention to people around him can come up with something that'll give us a lead."

He was still mulling that over when Jimmy and his mother showed up. The boy was a good half head taller than his mother and maybe an inch beyond his dad. His face was narrow, and he resembled the mother more than his dad yet looked very much a young man.

Hackett told his wife I wanted to talk with Jim alone.

"Why?" she asked.

I explained. She thought it over and glanced at Hackett. He shrugged, looking irritable.

"We could take a walk," said Jimmy.

Nobody objected, and we went outside and started north, past the crab apple trees, across the scruffy lawn, and along the edge of a wheat field.

I told him what I'd said to his father, and he listened, glancing my way a couple times but mostly looking ahead. A gopher watched our approach from the top of his clay-colored mound, then ducked into the hole with a flick of his tail.

"Do you or any of your friends have any notions who might've killed her?" I asked.

"Nobody's said anything I know of."

"Don't you talk about it?"

"No."

"How come? It'd seem the most natural thing in the world."

"Not to us."

"Why? Because everybody who knew her is so perfect you can't believe any of them could've done it? Or is it because she was so perfect it's impossible to believe anybody could do it to her?"

"Nobody's perfect."

"That's how I see it. So let's talk about just Gwendolen. She's gone, she can't be hurt anymore. What was there about her that'd make somebody go nuts and kill her?"

We came to a pile of rocks that had been gathered from nearby fields and piled in a small depression. Jimmy stopped and stared at them while I stood at his side, watching his smooth face.

"Well, she had a way of making you feel pretty stupid sometimes. I mean, she knew so many things, read such a mess of books, and was always wanting to talk about them. It wasn't so much showing off, it was like she thought she had to make you as smart as she was, and she got impatient when you didn't act like all that stuff was more important than real kids and this place where we live."

"Sort of like a missionary trying to convert the heathens, huh?"

"I suppose so, yeah, kind of like that."

"Did she want to be kissed?"

"I don't know, I never asked."

"You wait to be asked, it'll never happen."

He glanced at me, trying to look scornful, but didn't quite manage it.

I grinned at him. "I'm kidding you. The first time I got kissed, it was the girl's move. We were both only five. It was after my nose got broken and she felt sorry for me and kissed it and then my mouth. It was okay, because the nose was almost healed when she went for it."

He stared at me thoughtfully, then asked, "Did you kiss her back?"

"Sure. It seemed the polite thing to do."

"When was the next time?"

"About ten years later. Different girl. When'd you get your first?"

He looked away and said he didn't remember.

"I guess there've been a lot of them, huh?"

"Don't make fun of me."

"Okay, but don't bull-manure me. Stuff we're talking about, we don't forget. Did she make guys want to kiss her?"

"Well sure, she was pretty, what else makes guys want to kiss girls?"

"The way they treat you. The way they say and do things. Hell, just being around is usually enough unless they're nasty. Even then, sometimes, you want to—just to see if it might change them."

"Gwendolen wasn't nasty. She was just darned confusing sometimes—"

"That's what your friend Bobby said. He also claimed he never thought of kissing her. You believe that?"

"No, but he'd like to think it was so. She really managed to throw him."

"He was pretty crazy about her, huh?"

"It was nothing like that. I mean, he wanted to be important to her and he sure would like to have kissed her, but he'd never done anything to hurt her—never."

"How'd she like Hanson, the principal?"

"Not much. I mean, compared with Mr. Norberg or the

Bible school guy, Kilbride, he was a dumb jerk. Too big on himself to really see a girl like Gwendolen."

"She ever let him know it?"

"Not on your life. Gwendolen never let teachers know if she didn't like them. She was way too smart for that."

"You think she really kind of worked them?"

"I don't know. The fact is, talking about her this way seems stinky. She was a special kind of girl. Too special for the rest of us. It wasn't her fault none of us was smart enough for her. Sometimes that must've been darned hard. As soon as I heard what happened, it about made me crazy because I'd never got to know her better and never could now. It seems so lousy that a stranger can come to town and start digging up everything about Gwendolen, because some maniac killed her and worse. It's like even her memory is getting raped and murdered. . . ."

"You don't want whoever did this to get away with it, do you?"

"Of course not—"

"You want to leave the punishment to God—or the devil?"

"If I had my way, I'd cut the bastard's nuts off and kick him to death. But I just don't want her getting hurt beyond the grave in the hunt for him."

"Okay. That's understandable. But think about this whole business, and how it could have happened, will you? If you come up with something, let me know. Now let me ask one more question. You ever hear anything about how she got on with her brother, Sven?"

"I don't know. She never mentioned him that I remembered. She didn't talk about her family any, except sometimes her uncle Bjorn. She was proud of him. I don't think she had much of anything for her brother. They were just total opposites."

"But no fights you ever heard of?"

"No."

"How about her father, she talk about him?"

"Well, she let us know he was our doctor. That was about it."

"Did you ever hear she turned away from the religious thing in her last months?"

He stared at me. "No. I don't believe it, either. Where'd you hear that?"

"Her father told me so. She read some book that did it."

"I can't believe it. Shoot—she was a volunteer with the Bible school class, and crazy about old Kilbride and a whiz with the Bible. The doctor told you that? I guess maybe he was some jealous of Kilbride. Maybe she just let him think she wasn't into that anymore, to make him feel good."

It didn't seem he really believed that, but it wasn't something worth pushing. I thanked him for talking with me and left.

9

unday evening, a bit after seven, I strolled around to Abigail Smith's house and found Hazel Warford parked on the front porch chatting with her landlady. I ambled up and greeted the pair. Abigail, if she was charmed, managed to hide it well. Hazel smiled so warmly I invited her out for a walk. A moment later we were strolling toward the park.

"So," she said, "making any progress?"

"Nothing to brag about. Either with the murder or you."

"On the contrary, you're making fine progress with me. After the dance and all, I kept thinking about you well into the night."

"Yeah? You spend any of that time being sorry we didn't get cozier?"

"Some. But, silly as it probably sounds, I was feeling guilty about thinking I'd gained something from the tragedy of Gwen's death. If it hadn't been for that, we'd probably never have met."

"Did you always call her Gwen?"

"You know, that's funny. I never did. Neither did anyone else I know of. But now it just seems right. Isn't that weird?"

"Chris Kilbride would think it was improper. He corrected Officer Driscoll when he made the slip."

"Well, that's the missionary's way of putting people in their place. What's your impression of Chris at this point?"

"I'm not sure I can judge. He's too good-looking and smart for a guy like me to study with an open mind."

She grinned. "So, you'd like him to be a suspect?"

"I'd love it, but I can't figure how he could get back here from Wahpeton and not be noticed, coming or going. You know anything about how Gwendolen and her brother Sven got along?"

"Now, there you have a reason why Gwendolen hated her name shortened. It comes out sounding like her brother's. But to answer your question, I think they generally ignored each other. You could hardly get two people in one family more different. He's all tough guy, total male animal. He's so much of a man's man I've never heard of him having a regular girlfriend."

"What does he do?"

"He's been the janitor at the church all summer. Quite soon he'll be going back to the university in Brookings, where I think he's majoring in athletics. I'm not sure what kind, but am blamed sure it's not golf or tennis. Probably something like football. Do I detect a sudden gleam in your eye? Are you getting ideas about big brother working at the church and little sister being done in there?"

"Not me. I'd never think of anything that unnatural on my own. But now you bring it up—"

"No, I don't have any obvious reasons for getting ideas about incest. But it does happen, and it would seem to fit. Of course, it'd be a pretty awkward solution for you, what with his uncle having hired you to solve the case. How do you handle the possibilities?"

"Gingerly."

"Maybe you better ask for payment in advance."

"Can't. Our deal is, he pays me for any losses I have in sign painting because of my snooping, and he pays a wad if I come up with the killer. So far, I've not passed up any sign-painting offers and don't see any chance of nailing the killer. But there's something I'd like to poke into a little. Were there any of the guys or girls in school you think might've wanted to cut Gwendolen down? It seems to me the girls I talked to, just three of them, were a little too cute about not sounding antagonistic or annoyed with her, even though she worked at being the teacher's pet and was always putting classmates down. Do you know anything about how Becky Simpson, Kate Graff, and Zelda Johnson get on with each other?"

She frowned.

"I can't say yes or no, really. Zelda's the only one who ever hung around the library much. I wouldn't know if they saw each other outside of school or hung around each other in halls between classes. Have you talked with any of the boys who were in her class?"

"Yeah, Bobby Cartwright and Jimmy Hackett. They were both sweet on her but couldn't quite cope. Neither one of them are the kind to get her alone, and they probably wouldn't know what to do if they did."

"Did either of the boys say anything about how she got on with girls in their class?"

"Never thought to ask, and they didn't volunteer anything. Might be worth a shot."

"You always get along with kids?"

"Mostly, yeah. I've got two nephews, and we have fun."

She poked me for details and I gave her a few, including the business of teaching the younger one how to fight so he could get squared away with a class bully.

"But you've had no experience with little girls, huh?"

"I got adopted once by a four-year-old whose mom was killed in an auto accident. Actually it wasn't an accident. Some guys forced it."

"Tell me about it."

We were sitting at a picnic table in the park when I reeled off my story about four-year-old Alma, while Hazel sat beside me close, taking it in. When I finished she slipped her arm around my shoulder.

"How come you didn't have a gun?"

"Never was handy with one. They're a nuisance to carry anyway."

"And you can't really win a girl with one, right?"

"Never occurred to me."

I kissed her, and pretty quick we were wrestling with restraint and it was losing. She finally pulled partly free and said this was no place to go all out, and I said it beat the widow's boarding house, and she said not enough, so I suggested we get in my Model T and wheel out to my tent on the farm. For a minute it seemed she'd go for it, but then she got smart and said much as she liked the notion at the moment, she'd damned sure regret it later because somebody'd be bound to see us coming or going.

So she got her clothes rearranged, and we stood up and started walking.

"We'll do it eventually," she said, "but the circumstances have got to be better."

"Like where and when?"

"Well, you're a clever guy, you'll work up something. If you don't, I'll have to. Now I've got to get home before my reputation with the widow becomes fatally besmirched."

So we went back to the widow's and got briefly entangled on the porch before she pulled free and I walked home with an ache well south of my heart.

≪ 10 ≫

onday morning I went into town for a breakfast of pancakes, and while I was burying my stack in maple syrup, a lanky guy came by, said his name was Pinkerton and he understood I had painted the sign on Dugan's Drugstore. When I allowed he had me dead to rights, he grinned and said he needed something lots bigger, with bright colors. Could I handle that?

That sounded more promising than my chances of collecting $100 from Bjornson as a private snoop, so I asked for details. It turned out he owned the dance hall called Pinkerton's Pavilion. He admitted he'd originally wanted to call it a palace, but decided people might make fun since it wasn't exactly royal, and anyway, "pavilion" had a nice ring to it.

We drank coffee while discussing the project, then drifted around to his hall and got into location, size, and cost. The first two didn't take more than a few minutes, the third subject a lot longer. He had weird ideas about how much time and material was involved in a project as elaborate as he had in mind. This sign would be over the main entrance, a foot and a half high and eight feet wide. It was as ambitious as anything I'd ever done, and at least at that moment, Bjornson's niece and all that problem faded away.

After we'd agreed on the total bill and I'd promised to start the following morning, he went his way. As I was paying for my breakfast at the register, the cashier told me Pastor Bjornson had called and asked that I come to his house.

It wasn't ten yet when we were across from each other once more in his gloomy study.

"I hear you've been asking questions about Sven," he said without a greeting.

"You listen close, and you'll find out I've even asked questions about you. That's what happens in a case of murder."

He stared at me for a moment, then leaned forward to rest his elbows on the desktop.

"I hardly expected you to begin probing into the immediate family. That sort of thing is intolerable for a pastor in a community like this."

"A good percentage of killings are done by relatives and mates. The first thing a snoop has to do is eliminate the immediate family and move out from there. You want me to quit this case if I think maybe your nephew did it?"

"You think he did?"

"It's possible."

"But improbable."

"Could be. All I've done so far is try to cover every angle."

He stared at me for a moment, then nodded.

"Yes, I suppose so. I understand you have another distraction."

"Nobody works one job twenty-four hours a day."

"There is considerable talk about your involvement with Mrs. Warford."

"Mrs.?"

"Ah, you're surprised. Yes. She's separated, has been for some time, but she is married. I gather you didn't know that."

"Every day I find out there's more I don't know. So where's this hubby?"

"I'm not sure. Sioux Falls, I've heard. Wherever he is, he does exist, and it does not look well for you to be spending so much time with a married woman when you're supposedly investigating a murder."

"Okay, I'll keep that in mind. And I'll still be checking everybody that's connected with this case."

"All right—do what you have to do. I can't let this matter simply stand."

"There's another angle," I said, and told him of Pinkerton's job offer.

He stared at me and slowly leaned back.

"How long will this job take?"

"Maybe a couple days. I'll still have evenings, and once it's done, I can go back to full-time. This problem will keep."

"I suspect forever. Do as you will. My offer for the solution still stands."

I said fine, and went over to the widow Smith's house. She told me Miss Warford was at the school.

I found her in the library, which was a small room in a far corner on the second floor of Jonesville High School. She was stretching up to a top shelf, replacing a thin book.

If my greeting startled her, she didn't show it. Her smile was wide and warm.

"I've been talking with the pastor," I told her.

"Oh dear, this is so sudden," she said.

"He says you've got a husband."

The smile faded. "That's not quite accurate," she said, and walked around to the chair behind the nearby desk to sit down.

"How so?"

"I'm technically married, it's true. But we've been separated for over two years. It didn't seem like a terribly important thing to tell you about, since it's never occurred to me that you had honorable intentions. At least it didn't until you said you'd been talking with the pastor."

"It still seems like a thing you'd level with me on."

"All right, I should have. My marriage is the last thing I care to talk about. It was a stupid mistake—it's awkward, embarrassing, and everything else unpleasant. I try to forget it. You've been helping me do that, even in our very brief time together. Would you mind sitting down?"

I sat.

"Does it really make any difference to you?" she asked.

"It makes a difference to the pastor. He didn't make any threats, but I got the notion from his attitude that in this town folks wouldn't be too tickled to have their high school librarian messing around with a guy like me."

"They wouldn't be tickled even if I were single. In fact, they might be a little pleased to have the notion you were the wronged one in this situation."

"So tell me about the husband."

She took a deep breath. "All right. I met him while going to the university in Grand Forks, North Dakota. He was an assistant professor, and we got rather involved, and when I graduated we got married. That was three years ago this June. And I started teaching at Wilder School there, and Derek, my husband, was still with the university. We hired a Norwegian girl named Kari, who was fourteen, to come in and clean house, do dishes and things a couple days a week. And one day I became ill, left school early, and found Derek making love to our Kari on the couch. Kari wasn't feebleminded, but she was an extremely simple girl, and his taking advantage of such a kid made me madder than the notion of him cheating on me. I hit him on the head with the flat of a pancake pan and about knocked him silly. He threatened to kill me but was too stunned to get up. I left the house and never went back, not even to pick up my clothes. I made no secret of why I walked out. He lost his job at the university. Somehow he located me in Sioux Falls, and twice snuck into my apartment there and vandalized it. After the second time, the vandalizing was so vicious it scared me, and I moved without leaving a forwarding address, came here, and got a job waiting tables. Became friends with a customer who, when we got talking one afternoon, learned I was a college graduate with some teaching experience and helped get me my job at the school."

"Who was that?"

She looked at me for a moment, then glanced down at her hands folded on the desk.

"The Lutheran minister, Bjornson."

"You told him you'd been married?"

"I told him what I've told you."

I accepted that, and found the acceptance surprised me. Pastor Bjornson was becoming more and more interesting.

quatown was a half an hour's drive southwest of Jonesville. There I bought supplies for the Pinkerton sign, including lumber, hauled it back lashed to the right fenders, and stored the works in the pavilion basement. While driving through town, I'd spotted Becky Simpson and Kate Graff going into the soda shop, and right after unloading I hustled back in time to find them perched on wire-backed chairs at one of the round tables not far from the counter. They looked vaguely uncomfortable when I approached but made no objections as I pulled a chair over and joined them. Both were about down to the bottom of their sodas. I offered refills. Becky shook her head at first, but when Kate said, Why not? she changed her mind.

Kate was tall, with dark hair falling in waves to her shoulders. Her nose was straight and narrow as a Baptist's religious convictions, her mouth wide and thin-lipped, usually offering just a peek at her mostly even teeth.

Becky was half a head shorter, and very blond hair framed her round-cheeked face and full-lipped mouth. Her dimpled chin was a lot better looking than mine.

"Somebody told me," I said, "that you two were real close with Gwendolen in grade school but sort of drifted apart in the last couple years."

"Oh? Who said that?" asked Kate, looking innocent.

I grinned at her. "You and Becky aren't exactly high on my list of suspects, so don't get all shook up. I'm just trying to figure out what kind of a girl she was. What made her tick, you know? So far, it seems like she'd turned into a loner as she grew up, so I got wondering when it came out that for a while she had close friends in grade school. What changed her? Why'd she get murdered in that church basement? There's got to be some explanations. I'm just poking around until one shows up. And it just seems like you two might be able to tell me how she was different in high school from when she was younger."

The two girls looked at each other, and finally Becky turned to me.

"In high school she got all involved in reading thick books and talking about stuff in them, and after a while she made fun of us because we weren't interested."

"Was she interested in boys of your age?"

They both shook their heads.

"She was all full of Chris Kilbride and Mr. Norberg, or just about any of the teachers," said Kate.

"How'd she get on with her brother?"

Kate laughed. "She thought he was a total cretin."

"Did she hate him?"

"No. She told us he wasn't worth hating. She said that in junior high, I remember. Later on she said she didn't believe he was really her parents' son, that some unmarried mother probably left him on the doorstep in a cheap basket."

"You ever hear what he thought of her?"

Becky spoke up. "She said he'd told her uncle once that she'd never get a man until she lost her voice. Gwendolen thought that was pretty funny. Said it was the only time in his life he ever said anything almost clever."

"Did you ever go to a party with her, or double-date?"

"No. She wouldn't stoop to dating anybody in school," said Kate.

"Do you know if she ever met with anybody like Chris Kilbride, or Mr. Norberg?"

"You mean outside of school?"

"Yeah."

Kate shrugged, and Becky looked a little wise, but neither of them said yes.

Finally Kate said, "Who knows?"

"In this town, I thought everybody knew everything about everybody."

"Oh no, they don't," said Becky, with open satisfaction.

I couldn't get her to elaborate on that; she just insisted that it's always possible for people to hide things, even in Jonesville.

"If they couldn't," she said, "it wouldn't be any mystery about who killed Gwen."

I granted she had a point, then asked if they'd ever been close to Zelda Johnson. It wasn't really obvious, but both girls seemed to close up a little, especially Becky.

"What do you mean?" asked Kate.

"You get together any, to talk, or go out with guys?"

"Zelda doesn't go with guys," said Kate. "She says they're all dumb."

"How'd she get along with Gwen?"

"Well, they were pretty good friends in grade school and I guess even into junior high. By the time we were all in high school, she'd sort of pulled away from all of us."

"They were rivals in class, right?"

"You could say that."

"Who was brighter?"

"Well, who knows? The only thing plain was, Gwen made a bigger hit with teachers. She always let them know how smart *they* were. Zelda just wanted to show them how smart *she* was."

"Okay, let's get down to cases. Do you girls think Gwendolen ever really got close to Chris Kilbride? I'm talking about the two getting together in private and maybe getting really cozy. Doesn't that seem likely?"

"Yeah," said Kate.

"Probably," said Becky.

"And where'd that be, most likely?"

They looked at each other, then both shrugged.

"It'd be most likely in the church, where he taught, wouldn't it?"

"Probably," granted Kate. "But I can't quite imagine it at night."

"Well, it isn't like there's a steady stream of folks hiking that sidewalk or driving that street, right?"

They didn't argue with that.

"Weren't there any rumors about something like that?"

"Maybe some," said Kate.

"Didn't you talk about it between you?"

Becky looked worried, but Kate grinned. "Sure, what do you think?"

"You ever discuss it with Zelda?"

"Well, as a matter of fact," said Kate, "she was the one that raised the notion."

"What notion?"

"Just what you're getting at. That there was something going on between the two of them."

"Did she tell anybody else?"

The girls looked at each other, then at me.

"Probably not. She didn't really talk much to anybody else. To tell you the truth, I was a little surprised when she got sort of friendly with us."

"Has she been friendly since Gwendolen's death?"

They thought that over some and finally agreed they couldn't remember any times they'd got together with her since the murder.

"I guess maybe she felt a little guilty," said Becky. "Didn't want to talk about it."

"Even though it suggested she was right."

"Maybe that's why."

inkerton agreed to let me work on his sign in the pavilion, and I sanded and shaped up the backing with a good frame and laid on the sealer before suppertime. After eating I drifted over to the Johnsons' house and the missus let me in and said yes, Zelda was in her room, would I like to talk with her there? That seemed fine. She went up to check if she was decent, then called me up.

The room was what women call cozy and guys tag as dinky. Zelda had a single bed, a brown dressing table or vanity with triple mirrors, and a knee space between drawers. Her blond hair was freshly marcelled, her face had a scrubbed look, and her pale blue eyes were all innocence and sincerity.

She offered me the chair she was sitting on and moved to the edge of the bed, where she parked demurely with her feet close together on a small throw rug.

"You seem to have something in common with Gwendolen, besides being a good student," I said.

"Oh? What's that?"

"No close friends."

"Well, we couldn't help that. Ordinary kids just aren't comfortable with girls who make them feel dumb."

"I hear that back in grade school, Becky and Kate were pretty good friends with you as well as Gwendolen. What do you think of them now?"

"They're all right, I guess."

"What happened?"

"Well, they just never grew up much, not very smart."

"You think they resented you and Gwendolen dropping them?"

"I don't think so. They're not exactly terribly sensitive girls, you know. They may not even have noticed."

"I've heard rumors that Gwendolen maybe got cozy with the Bible teacher. Think there's anything to that?"

"Why not?"

"In this town it's hard to believe they could manage."

"Smart people can manage about anything, if they put their minds to it."

"And other smart people can spot it, right? Did you?"

"I didn't actually see anything, no."

"You know Kilbride's back in town?"

"Uh-huh. Dad saw him and told me."

"Know why he's here?"

She said she assumed it had something to do with the investigation of Gwendolen's death.

"You know he got an anonymous note right after she was killed?"

Her eyebrows went up. "How'd I know a thing like that?"

"If you happened to know somebody that wrote it."

"I don't. What'd it say?"

"It asked if he knew of her death."

"And that's all?"

"What else?"

She studied me for a moment and finally shook her head. "I can't imagine. Tell me."

"Can't."

"Or won't?"

"I heard you got a little chummy with Kate and Becky for a while last spring."

"I'd hardly call it that. We talked a little together when we shared an English lit class that semester. Becky was sitting behind me, and Kate was on my right."

"What'd you talk about?"

"Well, it was a class, after all, we didn't get into any real discussions. Maybe a word about the teacher, a question about the assignment. They talked more than I did."

"Who taught that class?"

"Miss Stewart."

"So she didn't squelch whispering the way Norberg did, huh?"

"Well, she didn't like it, but she wasn't as, you know, alert as Mr. Norberg. We could whisper things if she was busy at the board or got involved in talking with one of the other kids."

"You talked with the two girls outside of class some, didn't you."

"Sure, after class, or just before, if we happened to be close."

"You think Gwendolen really got into it with Chris Kilbride?"

She gave an innocent shrug. "I don't doubt she wanted to— but probably wasn't quite smart or nervy enough to manage. It's for sure Becky and Kate both wanted to believe something happened. They're great romantics."

"But you didn't encourage that idea?"

"Well, I certainly didn't go out of my way to argue against it. Why would I? We weren't ever that close."

"You think Chris Kilbride ever got involved with any other girls in around town?"

"I don't know that much about him, and just between us, I'm getting tired of talking about him."

Her mouth drooped at the corners, and it came to me that she'd been intensely jealous of Gwendolen, of her aggressive brightness, her great self-confidence, and how all of that had impressed Chris Kilbride.

"Well," I said, "don't let it get you down. With Gwendolen dead, there's no question about who's the smartest young girl in Jonesville, right?"

I meant it as a dig and was surprised when she grinned.

"Yeah," she said, "there's that."

13

The wind died at dusk, and there wasn't a sound but crickets chirping when I drove back to my tent and killed the engine. The nearby farmhouse was dark and still. I walked into the woods to take a leak before bed. An owl hooted in the distance. There was no moon, but the sky was so clear the glow of stars seemed bright enough to cast shadows.

As I was buttoning up, I heard the crackling of dried grass not far away and jerked my head to the right. There was nothing but deep shadows under the trees, and the crackling stopped. I used the trick of observing with side vision, which provides better sight in the dark, saw no movement, decided it must have been a raccoon or his like, and went back to my tent.

I was on the edge of sleep when the sound came again. I lifted my head and listened. Someone was walking up to the tent. The steps halted within a yard of my head.

"Good evening, Mr. Wilcox," said a deep, soft voice.

"Yeah," I answered, "who is it?"

"I could be your nemesis, if you try to come out, or even possibly your friend if you are wise enough to just listen and pay attention. Don't get up. Don't try to come out. I'm well aware that you're physically dangerous. I have a gun. If you come out, I'll shoot you. You understand?"

"That sounds real clear."

"Good. Are you aware that your lady friend Hazel is married?"

"Yeah. You her hubby?"

"A natural assumption. And quite correct. I've heard a great deal about you, Mr. Wilcox. They say you're very quick and strong. I'm sure you know that won't help against a bullet, and this gun holds six of them. I could hardly miss at such close range, so remember, the better part of valor is wisdom. Will you be wise and listen?"

"Why not?"

"Hazel," he said in a tone that sounded more sad than injured, "is rather fond of men of action. It's a surprising weakness in a woman so intelligent and seemingly sensible. When I discovered this fact, it seemed so out of character with the woman I thought I'd married, I simply refused to believe it at first. It took me some time to finally accept that she's a nymphomaniac. Didn't she surprise you?"

"No. I haven't been any closer to her than when we danced at the pavilion."

"Well now, Mr. Wilcox, that was pretty close, wasn't it? She rather likes to rub up against her partners, I'm sure you noticed. It's not a thing a man of spirit can overlook, right?"

"It wasn't that plain."

"Ah, you're going to claim she's become coy. Are you lying, Mr. Wilcox?"

"Would I lie to a man with a gun?"

"Probably. I'll admit, I would. Actually, Mr. Wilcox, I've come here tonight just to give you the true picture, and to warn you that I am not altogether sane where Hazel's concerned. She may be a nymphomaniac, but she is mine, and I intend to keep her. I won't tolerate a man like you taking advantage of her weakness. If you don't leave her alone, I'll kill you. If you don't believe me and see her again, ask her what happened to Harralson."

"Okay. Is her story about you doing the maid on the couch a lie?"

"Any story she has told about my unfaithfulness is untrue. This is typical of certain psychotic types. They accuse others of their own sins."

"Yeah, I've heard of that."

"Don't patronize me, Wilcox. You don't believe me, but you think about what I've told you, and remember my warning. Be sure to ask about Harralson. When she realizes you've learned the truth, she'll give you up and come back to Sioux Falls with me. That's all I'm after here. You stick to your sign painting and detecting, and with luck, you may die a natural death. Sweet dreams."

He moved off into the woods, and I guessed he had a car parked in the side road beyond. I slipped out of the tent, got to my feet, and listened until I heard a motor start in the distance and caught a flash of lights as he took off.

Then I went back inside and slept.

◁ 14 ⊳

The sign Pinkerton wanted was bigger than anything I'd done before and made me work harder than usual. Since I'm not the showman my sign-painting teacher Larry was, I worked inside. Larry had often drawn an audience, especially doing larger signs, and enjoyed standing back and squinting at his progress, making extra flourishes as he worked while pretending to ignore the gawkers. He worked faster than I could, but I followed his style of making shadowed effects on lettering, always in bright colors so it wouldn't look like I'd simply stenciled it all on the board.

When it was near noon I cleaned up, went over to the school, and found Hazel on her way to lunch at the café. It was plain her husband hadn't been in touch, since she looked fresh and high-spirited. She greeted me warmly and walked at my side telling of a student who'd fallen in love with Shelley's poetry.

When we were drinking coffee and waiting for our sandwiches, she suddenly ran down, frowned, and asked how come I was so quiet.

"Haven't had a chance to work in a word edgewise."

She laughed and confessed that she'd no doubt been carried away.

"So what're you doing, painting or detecting?"

"Just painting this morning. You heard anything from your ex in the last year?"

Her smile vanished. "No, why do you ask?"

"I think I've got bad news."

Her shoulders sagged for a second, then she leaned toward me.

"You've heard from him?"

"He came by my tent last night. I didn't see him, he stood outside and talked."

"Oh, God—"

"He said I should ask you about a guy named Harralson."

She took a deep breath and sat back.

"Did he threaten you?"

"Yeah. Was this Harralson guy a boyfriend?"

"He wanted to be. I met him almost a year after leaving Derek. Ted was his first name, he was really nice. I went out with him, maybe half a dozen times in as many weeks. And one night he was killed in a hit-and-run accident. That's what the news story called it. I got a call from Derek a week later. He said it was too bad about my boyfriend's death. I probably brought the poor man bad luck. He said he thought I'd be bad luck for any young man with big ambitions. That, on top of the break-ins I told you about, got me to come here."

"How do you think he found you?"

"I can't imagine. But he'd work at it. He's frighteningly persistent, very clever and obsessive—"

"Was Harralson the only guy you went with after leaving Derek?"

"The only one I went out with more than once. The fact is,

I wasn't really eager for a new man after Derek."

I asked what Derek did for a living now, and she said that after he lost his teaching job because of the girl, he made his summer job as a traveling salesman—peddling Electrolux vacuum cleaners, the last she heard—full-time.

"He's sold lots of things over the years, and I'm sure he makes out very well with lonely housewives."

"Why'd you come to Jonesville?"

"Pure impulse. When I walked out on Derek, I went to the bus depot and asked when the first bus would be leaving, and what towns it would hit. The fellow told me, and one of the towns he named was the same a friend of mine, who went through junior and senior years in high school with me, had come from. She had described it as a wonderfully peaceful little place, full of friendly people who, unlike in most small towns, minded their own business. She'd been too young to really know much about the character of the town, but it gave me romantic notions, and it just struck me as the last spot in the world anybody'd imagine me going to. I figured it was fate I should go there."

"So you bought the ticket."

"And got the job in the café the next morning. Maybe I should've realized it all went too easily to work out in the long run."

"What's Derek look like?"

"A movie star's best friend. He's got straight dark hair, which usually needs cutting, an ordinary nose, except maybe wider nostrils than average, a wide mouth with full lips, and a strong jaw. His cheeks are bony, his ears small with almost no lobe."

"Eyes?"

"Icy blue. With thick eyebrows that make one line across his forehead."

"Height and build?"

"Just under six feet, square shoulders and trim waist. Probably weighs about a hundred and sixty pounds."

"What kind of voice?"

"It's quite low, mostly. When he talks with strangers he's very formal, even stiff. A self-conscious style. It's one of the first things about him that began to bother me, he could sound so phony."

"Sounds like my visitor. He called me mister and said he might be my nemesis."

"Oh God, that's him all right. You're lucky he didn't kill you."

"Probably would have if he could figure out how to have a tree fall on me by accident. Guess I'll have to move into the hotel in town. Too easy to get at, out on the farm."

She agreed, and said we'd better not be seen together after this, until things got settled. Neither one of us could figure how he'd manage to keep up a surveillance without being conspicuous in a town as small as Jonesville. I asked for and got her promise that she wouldn't simply take off as she had before.

After some discussion I left the café ahead of her and walked up and down the block, taking in the half a dozen parked cars scattered about, eyeing the windows in the few buildings around with second-story windows that could be used for watching the street, and finally dropping into the open stores, looking at customers. There was no one remotely resembling Hazel's description of her hubby, and the cars all had local license plates.

Coming out of the soda fountain, I met Officer Driscoll and told him of my late-night visitor and his connection with Hazel. He didn't remember seeing any strangers in town, let alone the man she had described, but assured me he'd keep an eye out. He asked if Hazel had told police in Sioux Falls about the veiled threats made against her by Derek, and I said evidently not. She couldn't prove anything and was scared enough to take off immediately after his last call.

He said, "Women!" and shook his head.

I knocked off work on the sign about midafternoon, drove out to Sandstrom's farm, and broke camp. After packing my stuff I went up to tell the couple I was moving into town for a while and thanked them for their hospitality. They were big about it, said they'd miss me.

There was no problem getting a room at the Pickett Hotel; it wasn't doing any more business than the Wilcox Hotel in Corden. After settling in I went down to the lobby, called Hazel on the public telephone, and asked how she was doing. She said mostly she was stewing and thinking.

"What I've been thinking is, how Derek located me. He probably talked to people we both knew in Sioux Falls and might have stumbled across a hint, but I can't quite believe that. I suppose that since he's been traveling for several years, peddling all kinds of things, he probably has run into people who might have come across me—it's possible someone right here in Jonesville dealt with him before I ever came here. Maybe he had a housewife girlfriend, or lots of them, that he's been in touch with—"

"Your casual screwer isn't likely to want his women knowing where he lives," I said.

"I'm sure you're right. But he's a wonderfully creative liar. I suspect he provides every girl with a cozy history, probably about a comatose wife he cares for but can't make love to, or some other fairy tale to explain why he can't carry his new love off on his charger. He's the sort of man who'd want to hold on to every woman he handled, holding out false hopes that someday the two of them will be able to marry and live happily ever after."

"You got some basis for this notion?"

"After we split I remembered a telephone call I got one evening. It was a woman who asked who I was when I answered. I said Hazel, and she asked, oh, was I Derek's sister? and I said no, his wife. And she hung up. I don't know why that didn't make me suspicious at the time—I suppose I couldn't believe he was dumb enough to give a girlfriend his home number. Later on, I guessed she got the number indirectly."

We talked some more without educating me much, and I wished her good night.

At dusk I slipped out the hotel's side door and took a round-about way to Abigail Smith's house, where Hazel lived. The crossways streetlights at the corners were too dim to show up the house in the middle of the block. I walked past a wrought-iron fence belonging to her well-off neighbor, followed it to the back, and moved around an outbuilding that had probably been a car-riage house, built to cover a horse and buggy when the old maid's parents lived there. Beside it was a white outhouse, probably the cleanest in all history.

I checked inside. The only scent was a hint of something like bath powder Ma used in the past. It was a two-holer, which really got my imagination going, but nothing that came to mind seemed likely in this setting. I found an open door to the miniature barn and checked the place out. There was nobody below or in the small loft.

The hay door on the east side of the loft opened easily and silently. I took in the view, which mostly showed me the backyard of Miss Smith's west-side neighbors. If I got up near to the right edge, I could take in Miss Smith's back door.

I settled there till well past midnight, taking a couple breaks for a smoke inside where the glow wouldn't show for anybody scouting around outside.

A little after one I figured Derek wasn't going to show up, and I went to sleep on the haymow floor.

❈ 15 ❧

round four I woke, got up, and scouted the territory. Everything was peaceful as a Baptist church on New Year's Eve. I ambled back to the hotel and slept in until nearly nine. The mattress crackled with every move but was as comfortable as sleeping in my tent and easier to get up from.

While downing a breakfast of pancakes and coffee, I asked the counterman how long he'd been working in this café and he said about a year. No, he didn't remember any traveling salesman like the description of Derek that Hazel had given me. When the owner came around, he considered the description and said, yeah, he seemed to remember a dude like that a few years back. It was in the summer. A little after the Fourth of July, he thought. In fact, he might've been in town a couple times that summer. Or maybe there was a year between. He wasn't sure.

Somehow it was hard to put much faith in this guy's flexible recollector.

Out on the street I met Pastor Bjornson, who wanted to know if there was any progress in the Gwendolen case. I admitted it seemed to be stonewalled at the moment.

"Well, you have had a lot on your mind, haven't you?" he said. The words weren't directly critical, but the delivery suggested he wasn't approving.

"How soon," I asked, "will your nephew Sven be going back to college?"

"Classes start in October, but he'll be leaving a week or so ahead. He wants to look around for a part-time job and believes going early will give him a lead. Why do you ask?"

"I'd like to talk with him a little about his sister."

"You had a chance to talk with him when we first met. Why didn't you do it then?"

"At that time I didn't have any idea what to ask him. Now I need to know something about what he knew of her."

He didn't like any part of it but told me Sven would finish work at the church about four in the afternoon. Just before his quitting time, I walked into the church and found Sven in the basement putting cleaning equipment into a storage room. He didn't seem much excited by the sight of me.

I asked how he liked his job. He said it beat pitching manure, harvesting wheat, or digging ditches.

"You've done all that?"

"I worked on a harvest last fall. Why're you asking—you want my job when I leave?"

"Hadn't thought of it. What'd you think of your sister?"

"I never thought much about her. We didn't scrap, if that's what you're after. She was nuts about books and gab. I'm not."

"How about men?"

"What about them?"

"You think she got involved with them?"

"That was none of my business."

"You mean you didn't know or care whether she did?"

"What difference would it make?"

"Most brothers think it makes a lot of difference, the way their sisters behave and how the neighbors talk about them. Didn't anybody you know ever make remarks about her chasing the Bible school teacher, or her regular schoolteacher?"

"They wouldn't try it around me. Not more than once."

"Did anybody do it once?"

"No. They knew better."

"And you never cared whether she was messing around or not, as long as nobody dared blab about it to you."

"My sister minded her business, I minded mine."

"It doesn't figure, Sven. In a town this size, only a man deaf and blind doesn't know what's going on with his relatives, especially close as a sister. Something was going on, or she wouldn't have been murdered."

"You don't know that. She more'n likely got killed because she wouldn't put out."

"That's what I thought at first. And it could still be the answer. But it seems likely from what I've heard so far that she could easily have given some guys the wrong idea. I'm trying to nail which ones in town it could've been. You can't make like it has nothing to do with you. It seems like her own brother would be damned interested in getting to the bottom of it, and if you're not, it makes me suspicious. There've been cases where relatives of girls that messed around got so shook up they tried to put a stop to it, and things got out of hand."

"Come on, Wilcox, you think I'm so damned dumb I'd kill my sister to save the family honor?"

"You didn't like her, did you?"

"You got a sister?" he asked.

"Yeah."

"Older, younger?"

"Younger. Five years."

"Were you pals?"

"Yeah."

"Bullshit."

He was right in one way. Annabelle and I sure didn't chum about or even see each other a great deal. My old man doted on her and couldn't tolerate me, and it was pretty much the same with Ma. But Annabelle, from the time she was four or so, felt sorry for and defended me in her quiet, gentle way. I think it was the one thing she did that never failed to rattle Elihu. He couldn't figure out how this angel would want to comfort and support the devil's disciple in his household, but because she could do no wrong, it never occurred to him to criticize his darling. I think it only reinforced his conviction that she was a purely angelic child.

It didn't seem likely any of this would sound convincing to Sven, so I switched directions and asked if he'd known any of Gwendolen's friends at all.

"They're all kids, what the hell'd I have to do with them?"

"In this burg, you could hardly miss knowing them. Like Zelda, Becky, and Kate."

"I know about them—but none of them ever hung around our place, and if she ever mentioned them, it was just to make fun. Nobody was good enough for her except teachers, and not many of them."

"You hear her talk about anybody special?"

"Oh God yes, old Chris, the Holy Roller, mostly. At least for a while back last summer when she was his volunteer helper."

"You think he messed with her?"

"You mean did he make her? How'd I know? He might've, if he could get her alone someplace."

"Like in the church basement."

"Not likely."

"You work there, you see them together anytime outside the class schedule?"

"I sweep, dust, empty wastebaskets, and clean the cans. I don't keep track of the saints and sinners or do any spy duty."

"But you did work there last summer, when she helped with his class."

"I never caught him getting in her pants, okay?"

"Ever see them together?"

"Probably. I didn't keep notes and I wouldn't have given a shit if I had seen them gettin' cozy. It wouldn't have been anything to me."

"Even if it caused gossip?"

"You got it, detective. Now go give somebody else a pain, okay?"

"My problem is, I got this real strong hunch you had a thing about your sister. She put you down, pretty good, I think. And that church basement is home ground for you by now, and it just seems too likely that one of two things happened. You got her down there to tell her she was making a damn fool of herself over too many guys too old for her, or maybe you just decided you wanted to show her what a man you are, and you tried to lay her."

He hardly telegraphed the swing at all, but it was too much of a haymaker for real speed. I caught the fist with both hands and did my loop spin that wound him up facing the wall, with his hand in both of mine up his back. I slammed him against the wall and let go. He collapsed just fine, but right away got to his knees, then his feet, staggered, and made a dive for me. I slipped aside and caught him with a hook to the gut. He crumpled to the floor in a heap.

"You liked her when she was little, didn't you?" I said, crouching near his side, while keeping my right hand on his shoulder.

He moaned and held his arms tight against his middle.

"Did you worry about her?" I asked.

He muttered something I couldn't quite catch, but it sounded more like "Shit" than "Yes."

"Okay," I said. "I'm not going to talk about our little fracas here. If you don't, nobody'll ever know it happened. How's your forehead?"

He turned away, but I could see it was bruised from his contact with the wall.

"Think about things," I told him. "You can't just pretend she wasn't murdered. If you didn't do it, help me find out who did."

He took a deep breath, brought his right hand up, and touched his forehead, then his nose, and examined his hand. There was no blood. He leaned back and tilted his head against the wall at his back.

"You okay?" I asked.

"Just great," he said wearily. "I think you busted my gut."

"Guts don't bust. You'll get over it."

He shook his head and took another deep breath. When he let it out, he opened his eyes and stared at me.

"When we were just kids—I mean, she was six and I was eight—she thought I was big stuff because I was just about king of the playground at school. She hung around close whenever she could. It made me feel special, even though she was just a dumb little girl to my buddies then. One day my dad took me aside and said a boy shouldn't be too palsy with his own sister. I thought he was jealous, because she liked me better than him. But I didn't let her follow me around anymore, and by the time she was a freshman in high school, she didn't have any time for me anyway. She thought I was a dumbbell."

"That make you mad?"

"At first it just kind of threw me, then it made me mad, but finally I just sort of turned her off, you know? What the hell, outside of the house we never saw each other, and neither of us hung around there much once we got out of grade school."

"People have told me she admired your uncle a lot, and she made a big thing of her dad being the town doctor, but nobody suggests she cared much about him. You think she put him down the way she did you?"

"Well, he never had any time for either one of us. That really bothered Gwen. I think all the fancy reading she did, and the working like crazy for high grades, was supposed to impress him, but he never made a fuss about it or told her she was doing great."

"So she latched on to teachers and the missionary."

"Yeah. He did notice that. Got awful sick of talk about the preacher. He finally gave her a book a while back that seemed to shut her up."

"*The Age of Reason*?"

"Yeah, something like that."

"How's your gut?"

"Sore as hell. You ever lose a fight?"

"I can't afford to, I'm too little."

He didn't laugh.

"I've got one more question," I said.

He didn't look real interested.

"Where were you when Gwendolen died?"

He looked me straight in the eye. "I wasn't at the church. I'd finished by five and never went back that night."

"So where were you?"

"Well, you don't know when she died, do you, so how can I tell? I was probably asleep in my bed. That's where I always sleep when I'm not at school."

"What time did you go to bed?"

"Hell, I don't know. Maybe ten, ten-thirty, eleven. I don't punch a clock."

≼ 16 ≽

I went around to visit the doctor in his home. The timing was right—he wasn't off somewhere delivering a baby, he was parked in his living room with a very fat book. My visit didn't seem to surprise him any, and his wife, after answering the door and leading me to him, went back to the kitchen. I'd not seen him out of his white coat before, and the gray sweater seemed to shrink him some as he gazed at me from his easy chair in the corner while I sat on the side of the couch closest to him.

"That *War and Peace*?" I asked, nodding toward the book he'd lowered to the floor at his side.

His eyebrows went up. "Yes, it is. You're familiar with it?"

"Yeah. The librarian says your daughter read it. Does that belong to Hazel?"

"Hazel?"

"Warford. The librarian. She loaned her own copy to Gwendolen."

"Oh, of course. Gwendolen spoke about it to me when she'd finished it. Asked if I'd read it. I said something to the effect that it seemed far too bulky to be worth the time. It was the wrong thing to say. Her expression let me know she was offended. Now, suddenly, I seem to remember all too many occasions when, by some carelessly casual remark, I offended her. I find myself trying to find ways to make amends, and of course that's ridiculous, but I feel the need. For the first time in my life, I realize that my personal goals and commitments made me an incomplete father, and probably an inadequate husband as well— I don't know . . ." He shook his head, hopelessly, then asked, "Why are you here?"

"Still working for your brother-in-law. Looking for what your daughter was and what did her in."

"You think somehow it could have been my doing? That maybe, by my passive, even active neglect, I made her turn to others, looking for a loving father?"

"Could be."

He looked down at the book and shook his head. "I still think this is too blamed long."

"You read any novels you liked?"

"No." He sighed. "When you come right down to it, they're all lies."

"Where do you find the truth?"

He grimaced and shook his head. "I used to think it was in my profession. It still seems to be some of the time. But I'm not so sure anymore. Now I'm almost inclined to think the religious fanatics have it right. Forget about facts, clutch at faith and fantasy. We may be better off going crazy than being driven mad."

"How well do you know your son?"

He looked at me as if I'd just shown up and he hadn't heard me enter.

"Sven? That's an awful question to ask a father. I'm afraid he's as much a stranger to me as Gwendolen was. You might ask me how well I know my wife, Martha. I always thought I knew her perfectly well. Now I wonder. I look around, and for the first time realize I know more about my family's inner organs than I do about what's in their minds, what makes them live as they do. My one serious dialogue with Gwendolen in the last year had to do with her sudden passion for Christianity. We actually talked about that—or rather, I listened to her talk about it. And then I gave her Thomas Paine's *Age of Reason*. She never spoke of Christianity again, nor of Chris Kilbride." He shook his head in wonder. "I wiped out her delusions with one short book."

"Was she grateful?"

The look of wonder vanished, and he shook his head mournfully.

"No. What had liberated me simply deflated her balloon. Instead of thinking she'd learned the real truth, she only felt she'd lost something precious. When I asked her if she'd read the book I gave her, she said of course. What did she think of it? She said it was obviously all true. She made that sound like an accusation. When I tried to press her, she said she didn't care to talk about it, and left the room."

"You know if she wrote letters to Kilbride after he went back to Wahpeton, or had any other contact?"

"I've no idea." That seemed to depress him more than ever.

He suddenly lifted his head and called his wife. She came to the door and asked, "What?"

"Did Gwendolen ever get mail from Kilbride?"

"I don't remember any letters. But most of the time she picked up the mail, so I couldn't be sure. She never mentioned anything. . . .Why?"

"Never mind. It's just something that came up while we were talking. You want to bring us some coffee?"

She went back into the kitchen.

"She'd never notice anything. In her mind, Gwendolen could do no wrong."

"But you knew better?"

He flushed. "I didn't say anything like that. The difference here is that I kept some perspective in dealing with your children. A man knows very well his children are human. Mothers think they're angels—especially if they're girls."

"One other thing, Doc. Where were you the night Gwendolen died?"

His chin didn't quite drop, but it sagged a moment before his eyebrows went up.

"Well," he said after a moment, "I believe I was at Bushaw's farm, delivering their baby son."

"What time did you get back home?"

"It was about ten-thirty or eleven." He sat up a bit and called, "Martha!"

She came to the door.

"Mr. Wilcox asked me when I got home the night Gwendolen died—I told him it was between ten-thirty and eleven. Wasn't that it?"

She looked at me and said yes, just about.

17

y next move was to the high school, where the principal told me the English teacher lived in Summit, about twenty-five miles away.

"Owns a small house there, left to her by her departed parents."

He gave me directions and I took off.

Summit was less than an hour away, and the view looking north of town, which gives you the feeling you can see all the way to Canada, has always grabbed me, so the trip was welcome. Miss Stewart was seated in a wicker chair on the porch, facing east, and watched my approach with unblinking, watery blue eyes as I parked in front and strolled the walk to meet her. She lowered a folded newspaper, revealing the crossword puzzle she'd been working on.

"Miss Stewart?" I asked.

"How did you know?"

"This is the address I was told you lived at."

"Somehow I don't think you're a salesman."

"You got that right. I'm Carl Wilcox, working for Pastor Bjornson. I guess you know him."

"A safe presumption. So you're the one trying to find out who killed Gwendolen. I gather you've not made much progress."

"Sometimes that's hard to measure, but I could sure use any help I can get."

"If you step inside there, you'll find a small wicker chair to the right in the living room. Why don't you bring it out and sit down?"

I did. She smiled. It was a most kindly smile, but at the same time there was an air of examination and evaluation in her manner that most likely kept students in their places anytime she occupied a classroom.

"Did you learn anything about Gwendolen in your classes that'd give a hint why somebody might want to kill her?"

"I'm sorry to say, yes. She was too clever, too self-confident, and often overbearing. Some of the boys were overawed, a few were simply cowed, and many of the girls quietly despised her."

"Was Zelda one of the despisers?"

"Well, she certainly wasn't fond of her, but I can't quite picture her strangling Gwendolen, who was almost half again her size."

"Maybe she had a big, strong friend."

"None that I can think of. She doesn't like boys. Actually, you'd almost think she didn't like anyone. A very private girl."

"Except this last spring she got friendly with two classmates, Becky and Kate."

Miss Stewart's eyebrows rose a fraction, and she tilted her head back. "Well, well. You have been doing your homework, haven't you? Yes, I noticed them whispering now and then, early in the second semester when they huddled in the hall outside my room a few times. It surprised me. They're very unlikely types for her. I finally assumed she decided to mix a little with the simple folk, perhaps to reassure herself of her superiority."

"But she never talked with Gwendolen?"

"Not that I know of. They were born antagonists. I suspect Zelda is every bit as intelligent as Gwendolen was, but she felt dwarfed, I think, at least physically, and couldn't make herself play up to teachers, or any adults for that matter, the way Gwendolen did so naturally."

"Was Sven ever a student of yours?"

"Oh yes. Actually, he's more intelligent than he cares to let on. The few essays I demanded from his class showed me he could think and even organize, but he was careless and not really interested in literature. I suspect he was put off in part because his sister was such an avid reader and got so much from books. He couldn't begin to compete. It's very difficult for an older brother to accept gracefully that his little sister can outdo him at anything at all."

"Did you hear any talk about Gwendolen getting cozy with her men teachers, or the Bible school guy?"

"I heard murmurings now and then about her being terribly forward. Never took them seriously. She was a young woman stimulated by older people, men and women. I don't think there was anything unnatural about her, or that she was overly precocious romantically. She wanted to dazzle the world, win admiration and approval. That's not the sort of girl who gets herself into compromising or vulnerable relationships."

"Do you know her father, the doctor?"

"Only by reputation. I understand he's most competent; understanding with adults, rather assertive with children, perhaps a bit aloof. I rather suspect Gwendolen's pursuit of approval and attention from adults in the school system was to compensate for a kind of neglect at home."

"You think about your students a lot, don't you?"

"Yes, I'm afraid I do. I like to think it makes me a better teacher if I can work inside their heads a little, get some notion of what makes them think and work the way they do. There are too many to do a really effective job with, and some, frankly, simply aren't interesting enough to work on much. And if you tell anybody any of this, I'll call you a liar."

I grinned at her, and after a moment, she grinned back.

"Your father didn't approve of you, did he?" she said.

"He still doesn't. Maybe more than ever."

"But you've compensated."

"I like to think I've thrived on disapproval."

I asked for her opinion of Chris Kilbride, and she frowned thoughtfully.

"From all I've heard, he seems almost too good to be true. Evidently the children in his classes worship him. I've only seen him a few times and never heard him talk, so there's no way for me to judge anything beyond the fact he looks the part I hear he plays; an inspiring, maybe even saintly, young man. You have a little problem accepting that, don't you?"

"Well, you just said he sounded too good to be true."

She smiled. "Not quite. I said he seemed *almost* to be that. You can accuse me of hedging, but that's all."

When I thanked her for talking with me, she said it had been a pleasure and smiled as though she really meant it.

18

The truck appeared behind me about a mile outside of Summit. It was pretty easy to ignore until a bit later, when it became evident it was coming on in a rush, and the driver paid absolutely no attention to the thick dust cloud my flivver was raising between us. Since he was obviously in a great hurry and I wasn't, I eased up to let him by. He made no attempt to pass, just stayed on my tail for a couple miles, and at first I figured the dust up close was too much for him, but that didn't make sense when he stayed so tight, and I began wondering. When we topped a low hill and headed down toward a bend along the side of a steep slope, he pulled out, sped up, and began coming alongside.

I hit the brakes.

As the car began skidding, I saw the truck fender moving just past my front wheels and closing in. By this time I'd slowed the Model T a tad, so when it hit the ditch I was able to straighten enough to keep from heading down the slope, but not enough to keep from turning over. I ducked over the wheel, hanging on with both hands, protecting my face, felt the jolt, and heard shattering glass and crunching metal.

The next moment I was climbing out the sprung door and watching the truck skid along the ditch edge. It wavered a moment, then pulled back on the gravel and wheeled on.

I was alone with my wrecked car and a great view of the prairie off to the west.

❖ 19 ❖

man in a new black Buick spotted me by the wreck about half an hour after my arranged accident and gave me a ride into Jonesville. It was pretty plain he wasn't convinced by my story. He kept sniffing, trying to catch a whiff of booze on my breath. When I asked him to let me off at City Hall, he obliged, wished me good luck, and wheeled away like a man happy to be set free.

Officer Driscoll took in my tale with a growing grin that made it plain he got a kick out of me running into more than I could handle. He agreed it was likely the truck driver had been Hazel's husband, Derek Warford. While I was trying to figure how to replace the Model T, somebody called Driscoll and reported a stolen truck. It was abandoned on a dirt rut road about half a dozen miles from Jonesville, where a farmer found it blocking his way to a pasture. Driscoll took off to check it out.

I went to the library and talked with Hazel.

"How the hell does he manage it?" I asked. "The son of a bitch can't be invisible, and he can't fly, but he seems to get anywhere and everywhere without being seen."

"He won't do anything again until you've begun to forget about him," she said. "That's how he operates. I can't imagine how I ever got involved with such a spook, but you've got to admit, he's original and imaginative."

"Oh, I don't know—he gets in ruts. Trying to manage another hit-and-run. He ought to come up with something new."

She shuddered. "That's just what I'm afraid of. I just can't run again, and I know you won't. You need a gun, you know? You can't just keep surviving against him bare-handed."

"Don't think it'd make any difference. He's never manhandled you, has he?"

"No. He never even got mad in a way that showed, except when I hit him with the pancake iron."

"So maybe I don't have to worry about him damaging you personally."

"He'll have no qualms about harming you."

"But he wants to make it look like an accident. Like with the boyfriend. You know if he ever owned a gun?"

"Not when we lived together."

"So he was probably lying when he said he had one the night he came to my tent."

She agreed.

"But that doesn't mean he's not dangerous. I've no question but what he'd set the hotel on fire if he thought it would kill you, or even just scare me silly. We've got to get away—"

"Can't right now. Won't have a stash until I finish Pinkerton's sign, or nail Gwendolen's killer. If I could do that, we'd be set."

She looked at me and shook her head. "No. You'd rather die than run. And you think he won't hurt me, so you don't worry about that."

"What we need to do," I said, "is get you out of Abigail's

place. You're right, I don't figure Derek's going to hit you, but he's hit places you've lived, and he might even hit your landlady. Maybe we'd ought to move you to the hotel, where it wouldn't be so easy for him to operate as around that house in the dark."

"You think I'd be safer if I moved in with you?"

"Well, if he's as tough as you think, it might give me some dandy last days and nights while I lasted."

For a second it wasn't plain whether she was going to laugh or cry, but instead she just shook her head and put her chin in her hands.

"I don't know. Every time I think I'm beginning to really figure you out, you pull a switch on me. You never seem genuinely concerned about anything. You don't know the meaning of fear, do you? Except maybe about being trapped—but I'm not even sure of that. You've taken on this Gwendolen thing and you'd rather die than give it up, wouldn't you? Is it the same with me? Am I another goal?"

I pulled a chair from beside the wall, put it beside her desk, and sat down.

"Mostly," I said, "I take what comes. It isn't a matter of adding up scores or building a record. The best times I've known happened when I was lucky enough to square accounts, and the other times when I got to know a woman worth knowing and we enjoyed each other. Getting married when I did was my biggest mistake. Strictly stupid. She played a fiddle. Was good at it, loved having an audience, the bigger the better. That's what she lived for, a whole mess of people out there admiring her, never seeing her except on show, not knowing a damned thing about her except the sounds that came from that box, those strings, and a bow. She never wanted to be real. Why in the hell we got together I'll never know, it just happened one night when everybody was drunk and we went to bed together and she said we had to marry, and what the hell, I'd always thought I'd try anything once. Then she wanted me to go onstage with my lariat. I squelched that and brought her to South Dakota, and she lasted a week. Greatest relief in my life when she took a train back east."

"So you went on the bum and never quit?"

"Well, I haven't been riding the rails for quite a spell now, and I've never really panhandled. Maybe accepted free drinks from a lucky bum along the way, but not lately. Enough ancient history—how about you try to help me figure out just where the hell your hubby's hiding out, and how he manages to keep an eye on me. There has to be some kind of program he's working."

"All I can suggest is what I told you before. He's probably hanging out with some former customer he seduced."

"It'd almost have to be somebody living within sight of the hotel. A place where he could see me pull out and then follow me."

"Maybe he knows someone in the hotel."

I tried to remember any of the other guests, or even the people who worked there, and realized they were all strangers, since I hadn't been around the place long enough to catch sight of the hired help.

She finally agreed on moving to the hotel because she was genuinely concerned about Abigail being the loser if she stayed with her. There didn't seem to be any percentage in trying to be sneaky about the move—it would be impossible to keep it a secret—so I went home with her, she packed a suitcase, and we walked back and signed her in.

The proprietor, Jud Pickett, a man between middle and old age with a bony body and a small potbelly, agreed to put her in a room across the hall from mine. He didn't raise his eyebrows or ask any questions. While Hazel began unpacking her clothes and getting settled, I went downstairs with Pickett and asked if he had any fairly recent guests who'd been staying a few days.

He didn't.

I described Derek and asked if he remembered such a guy from the recent past.

He gave it some thought, asked if I knew what the guy peddled. I said vacuum cleaners, among other things.

"Yeah, rings a bell somewhere. Probably four or five years ago. Kind that's always selling, products or himself. Never a letup. He had the hired help climbing all over each other to get his attention. Name was something like Dirk, I think."

"Derek Warford?"

"Yeah, that sounds right. Could be it."

"Any of the help from then still with you?"

The grin, which had been broadening, faded.

" 'Fraid not. We can't pay enough to keep help that's really good for very long. They get married or go to school someplace, get a better-paying job."

"How about your cook?"

"Well, yeah, she's been with me five or six years. But she was never cozy with the hired girls and doesn't meet the guests."

"Can you name one or two hired hands that were with you when Derek was around that I might find in town?"

"Yeah, Dora Lynne's still here. Has a beauty shop in her apartment, kitty-corner from us on Main. Second floor of the Cooper Building, over the soda fountain and Elroy's Hardware."

"Married?"

"No. Somehow never made a connection. Don't know why, she's not that bad looking, kinda nice shape, I mean, not too fat or skinny. Too shy, I guess."

I thanked him for his help, went out in the front sidewalk, and looked toward the Cooper Building. It was a two-story, flat-roofed place with narrow white siding, and the corner windows of the second floor overlooked Main Street and First Avenue.

The stairway to the second floor was on the corner, and I went up the creaking steps and found the beauty salon behind the first door on the right. Looking through the glass door, I could see something like a barber's chair and a young woman working on a matronly type who was draped with a white cloth. A hall ran the length of the outside wall, and I followed the black rubber liner and looked out in the alley, where parking space was available but empty. There was a door next to the back entrance, evidently access to the apartment behind the beauty salon. I was tempted to try entering but resisted, walked back to the front, and looked into the salon again. The matronly lady was ponderously getting out of the chair while the beauty operator stood with her back to me, blocking the patron's view. I quietly went down the steps, returned to the hotel, and went up to Hazel's room.

"How'd you like to get your hair done?" I asked when she answered my knock.

"What's wrong with it?"

"Nothing. But there's this beauty parlor lady who may know Derek. It'd probably work better if you talked to her than if I tried it. It's not likely she gives men haircuts."

Hazel liked the idea. She went down to the lobby and, after checking the phone book, gave the lady a call. She got an appointment for a half an hour later, and we spent the waiting time going over her line of questioning.

When she showed up back at the hotel after keeping her appointment, her hair was a bit overwaved for my taste but looked okay, and she was obviously feeling pretty self-satisfied. We went to dinner in the hotel restaurant, and she gave her report.

"My first impression was that she's older than she looks—her face is plain but not homely, and her figure is okay. She's a girl who never turns heads, one way or the other. Once she knew what I wanted, she asked casual questions about my work at the school and where I'd come from before moving here. When I asked questions, she was very politely evasive. I told her I'd heard of her from the hotel man and asked how she'd liked working for him. She said he was okay, but his cook was something of a pain. Too bossy and impatient. Asked me not to quote her—not that it would make any difference, since the woman never had her hair done in her life.

"I asked if she ever met any interesting people while working there. She said there were a few, and mentioned a woman who was very fat and awfully nice and sold beauty supplies. I asked what about fellows and she said they were either too old and bossy or too young and fresh."

Since the subtle approach got her nowhere, Hazel finally said she'd known a man once who traveled in this territory, and asked if she was at the hotel when Derek Warford came around. After a short pause, Dora said no, that name wasn't familiar. There had been too many people to remember them all.

"You believe her?" I asked.

"No. I don't for a moment believe if Derek were around, she wouldn't have noticed him. When I told her he'd been my husband, she just said, 'Really? Did he die?' I said no, I walked out on him because he made love to a fourteen-year-old girl on my couch in our home, and I caught him at it. I looked around at her when I said that, and she turned red and muttered something like, 'How awful—' and it was plain she didn't believe me. He's no doubt told her the same story he told you, that *I* was the philanderer. And then I told her what had happened to Harralson and to you and asked her if the truck he ran you off the road with had been kept parked in back of her place the day he saw you leave town, when he watched from her window. She said she had no idea what I was talking about, but she struck me as overly defensive. Do you think maybe we could talk with the cook she mentioned working with at the hotel? If it's still the same woman, she might know if Dora ever got involved with one of the guests."

It seemed worth a shot.

20

We found Jud in the lobby, and I asked him to introduce us to his cook. He had to know why, took in my story, and finally agreed. Before he led us down a back hall toward the kitchen, he volunteered some background.

"Her name's Purita, short for Purification. She's Spanish. Probably the only Spaniard in South Dakota—certainly the only one I know of. Came here from the east after answering an ad for a wife. The joker who sent for her never showed up at the train— or if he did, one look at her was enough to squelch the offer. She took a room here, and it just happened I was having trouble with the cook on duty, and when I learned Purita had been a cook in New York, I offered her the job. She's been here ever since. A damn good woman."

I expected her to be fat as Bertha at the Wilcox Hotel. Instead she was tall and slender, with big dark eyes, furry brows, and a wide, full-lipped mouth over a chin a little too big.

Jud introduced us. She gave Hazel a glance and turned her dark eyes on me as her boss explained what we were there for.

"Want a cup of coffee?" she asked me.

"Why not?"

She moved easily despite her height, took three cups from a shelf, poured from the big blue pot sitting on the range and waved us over to a small table in the kitchen's northeast corner, where we sat in creaky wooden chairs.

"You remember a guest named Derek Warford?" I asked.

"Never saw him. Heard the name, though." She glanced at Hazel. "Same last one as yours."

"He was my husband. Still is, actually. We've been separated for years."

"Run out on you?"

"I walked out when I caught him making love to our cleaning girl."

The dark eyes took on a gentler cast as she nodded.

"Was Derek around," I asked, "while Dora Lynne worked here?"

She nodded again, returning her gaze to me.

"You know if she got to know him?"

"She waited on him in the dining room. Cleaned his room, changed the sheets. I don't know if she helped dirty them or not. I'm not a second-floor woman."

"She ever talk about him?"

"Not to me. Did to her partner, though. They both thought he was a caballero. Very handsome."

"Who was the partner?"

"May Banks."

No, she wasn't still around. Married a local boy, and they moved to California.

That was about all I could get from her. She wouldn't, or couldn't, be any more specific about Dora Lynne's involvement with Warford. But she was certain the two maids had talked of the man several times and even suspected they had competed for his attentions. She couldn't offer anything more substantial than overheard gossip between the two women.

After a short conference on the sidewalk in front of the hotel, Hazel agreed we should confront Dora Lynne. The beauty shop door was locked, and no one answered my knocking there or at the rear door. We promptly hiked over to City Hall, found Driscoll, explained what we'd been up to, and tried to persuade him to get us into the apartment to check on Dora Lynne. He refused, saying there weren't grounds enough for a search at this stage. My argument that this bastard was probably crazy enough to kill the girl if he thought she might be used in making a case against him didn't sell. He said if she hadn't shown up by the next day or so, maybe he'd bust in.

"I don't believe Derek's done anything awful to her," Hazel told me as we walked back to the hotel.

"So where is she?"

"I think he's told her more tall tales and frightened her into hiding. He's been very careful not to do anything that could be easily traced to him. I mean, the damage to my apartment, the killing of Harralson, they would be hard to really pin him down on. It's even possible the hit-and-run was a genuine accident. The fact that Derek implied it wasn't is no proof. He's the biggest opportunist I've ever known."

"Him trying to run me off the road and wrecking my Model T was no accident. This guy's a nut, and there's no telling what direction the nuttiness will go in."

"You want me to be afraid?" she asked.

"I don't want you making any fatal mistakes."

"Well, I've taken your advice and moved to the hotel. You think I'll be safe in a room across the hall from you?"

"You'll be safer from Derek."

"Maybe I'd be even safer if you shared the room with me."

"Now, why didn't I think of that?"

"I suspect you had it in mind from the start. Have you got a rubber?"

"No."

"So now I have to decide whether you said that because it's true, or whether you just don't want me to believe you were taking anything for granted, or worst of all, whether you just don't worry about what happens as long as you have your fun."

"I hardly ever take anything for granted, especially since I met you, and much as it hurts, I can manage to pull out before it's too late."

"That's a high-risk technique, and you must know it. How about we pull it off with mutual massage?"

"That's not a bad term. It'd beat total frustration."

It did. It beat the hell out of it, and that's all I'm going to tell you on the subject.

Well, I'll admit one more thing. I made up my mind I'd buy a supply of rubbers the first chance I got.

21

I've probably never been more discombobulated than I was the next morning. It was bad enough finding myself so stuck on a woman that nothing else seemed worth bothering about, but the worst part was, it forced me to think I had to get organized to keep this thing going, and I'd never been more fouled up in my life.

First, I was near broke, and second, the Model T, which had been my portable home, workshop, and supply station, had been wiped out, along with a good share of my working gear.

So after a rush breakfast with Hazel in the hotel, I ran down Pinkerton and laid out our common problem. Without my rig and equipment, there was no way to finish his sign. He took it all in, nodding now and then, and without any diddling around agreed to give me a ride to Aquatown, plus a loan to cover the cost of my replacements. He assured me he had business in the big town and was glad to take me there.

Since I never lost sight of my number-one item of business, my first stop was in a drugstore for a package of Trojan rubbers. After that I hit used car lots and finally located an old Model T that a local mechanic had converted into something like a pickup truck and hadn't been able to sell, so the price was right. It had a back I could put a top on and convert into a combination equipment storehouse and emergency bunk. None of my brushes had been messed up too much in the wreck, but I had to restock some paints, thinner, and other necessities.

Pinkerton met me for lunch and told a lot more about running a dance hall than I wanted to know. Luckily he was the kind of guy who doesn't notice if you don't seem to be taking notes on his line, and through most of his blather I thought about Hazel.

We got back to Jonesville by midafternoon, and I went around to the school and found her at her desk. She was pleased to hear of my success with Pinkerton, and looked a little smug when she said she had another encouraging note for me.

"I talked with Pastor Bjornson about your problems. He's very sympathetic and says he'll advance you twenty-five dollars to help meet expenses caused by your car being wrecked. I'm afraid I wasn't altogether honest with him about what caused the accident—just sort of hinted it might have been someone trying to stop your investigation."

"But you didn't say which investigation?"

"It slipped my mind there was more than one."

"It's a good thing one of us is able to keep level, what with all the distractions. Which reminds me, I got a supply of what you told me I needed."

"Are you suggesting it wasn't just rubbers that inspired you to go shopping in the big city?"

"I hope Pinkerton thinks so. You haven't received a little note or anything from your hubby, have you?"

Her big smile faded some. "No. Nothing. And in case you're wondering, the hairdresser hasn't been back to her parlor. Or at least not by this noon, when I checked."

I shook my head. "This is the first time I've ever had an assistant. You're going to spoil me."

"Well now, I rather thought of myself as a partner, not an assistant. And I don't mean a silent partner."

"How about we go over to the hotel and have a conference, partner?"

"That's just about an irresistible offer, but it might be bad for business in the long run. People are going to be talking enough about us having rooms across from each other at the hotel. If we start meeting there afternoons, the racket could be deafening."

I was ready to risk it, but didn't think she could be persuaded and suggested we go have supper and discuss our next steps.

The discussion got pretty involved, and some of it was actually about the Gwendolen thing. A little more covered Derek and the dangers he offered, but eventually Hazel got into the subject of a visit to Corden and the Wilcox Hotel, and her meeting my parents and Bertha. I had trouble with that notion. It was for sure my old man, Elihu, would be knocked out by her, while at the same time assuming I must have hypnotized her some way before she could possibly have got herself involved with such a bum. Ma would probably think Hazel was too good for me too. It'd be a little messy having both parents knock me to a woman I'd tumbled for.

It seemed like a time to switch subjects, and I told her maybe we ought to concentrate on the Gwendolen murder. She said not yet, she had more news about Derek.

"I talked this morning with Miss Stewart. She remembers having Dora Lynne in her English class six years ago. Says Dora's family moved to Yankton just after she graduated. That was the year she went to work at the hotel, and she stayed in Jonesville, since she was getting room and board and wasn't that excited about leaving a town, where she'd gone to school and knew lots of people. The sad thing is, from what checking I've done, she never really got close to many of the townfolk, but she started the beauty parlor after working a year for Mrs. Beadle as a beautician, and surprisingly, she ssems to have made a go of it. That makes it hard for me to believe she'd voluntarily give up her business and simply take off."

"We better call the parents, see if they've heard anything."

"Ah, great minds do run in the same channels—I called just an hour ago. They heard from her yesterday. She told her parents she was marrying a man from Sioux Falls and had left Jonesville for good. She'd be in touch."

"Name the man?"

"Uh-huh. Daniel Warrick."

"Sure. As in Derek Warford, huh?"

"That's what I figured."

"So maybe you're right, he hasn't killed her. It sure doesn't get him located."

"No, but it may distract him for a while. That's probably the whole reason he talked her into leaving with him. It gives him something to do while he waits a week or so before making another move on me. That sounds awfully self-centered, I know, but it's the way he operates. He likes to build suspense. Like the way he waited a week before calling me about the hit-and-run."

"So we better get the Gwendolen business settled before he shows up again."

"You make it sound simple. Okay, what do we do?"

Nothing brilliant came to mind, so I suggested we go to the soda fountain for fudge sundae desserts, and she snapped it up.

The nice thing about small towns is that you're always running into people you know. We found Zelda sitting at a corner booth in back of the fountain and moved in on her. She didn't look too thrilled but managed to be polite and almost smiled when Hazel noticed the book she was reading, *Silas Marner* by George Eliot.

"That's a pen name for an English woman named Mary Ann Evans, who wrote lots of books in the mid—eighteen hundreds."

"Did Miss Stewart recommend it?" asked Hazel.

"Yes."

"How do you like it?"

"It's very interesting." She gave me a wise look. "It begins with talk about wandering men, peddlers, knife grinders, weavers. How they raised superstitious fears with rural people, because they seemed homeless and unnatural. The locals thought these men wandering the land must be evil, and maybe know too much. Imagine if she were writing about a man like you instead of Silas Marner."

"Hard to picture," I said.

"Not for me."

"All of our ancestors were wanderers," said Hazel. "Isn't it strange that the Indians, in the beginning, seemed to welcome the wandering white men?"

"Maybe it was because Indians were mostly wanderers too," said Zelda, "at least the Plains Indians were. They probably felt something in common with strangers."

They looked at each other with something like surprised approval.

"What a striking coincidence," said Hazel, "that you'd happen to be reading this book at this time. When did Miss Stewart suggest this to you?"

"It was on a list of books she handed to us in class at the beginning of last year. I just never got around to it till now."

"Do you think people in Jonesville are like the peasants Eliot wrote about?"

"A little, yes. Oh, they're not *afraid* of peddlers and such, but they don't think of them as normal people, you know? They're not like, say, black or yellow, but they don't really belong either."

"What about priests and ministers? They're usually from outside, but they're generally accepted, aren't they?"

"Well, sure, especially ones like Pastor Bjornson, who have families and stay around a long time. Any priest is accepted because, after all, he's sent straight from God, or at least that's what Catholics seem to believe."

Hazel laughed, and Zelda's smile widened.

"Tell me," Hazel said, "I'm a relative newcomer in town—do you think I'm accepted?"

"Not really. I mean, you haven't gotten close to anybody, don't have any relatives in town. It's nothing against you, it's just the way things are. That's why you two have got together, don't you think?"

Hazel looked at me, still smiling, and agreed that might have a lot to do with it. Then she leaned forward and sobered.

"Are people talking about us?"

"Well, what did you expect? You moving into the hotel—"

"Have you heard why?"

"Well, it seems plain enough."

"You know I'm married?"

"So they say."

"And that my husband has been making trouble for me?"

"I haven't heard anything about that. What's he done?"

Hazel told her. Beginning with the reason why she deserted her husband and concluding with an account of the visit I had at the Sandstroms' farm and the wrecking of my car.

Zelda took it all in with wide eyes that occasionally flickered my way but mostly stayed on Hazel.

"Do you think," asked Zelda, "that maybe it's your husband who killed Gwendolen?"

"That never occurred to me. How'd he meet her?"

"Well, I don't have any idea, but if he's been around and they somehow met, it could've happened. You said he was making love to a fourteen-year-old girl in your home. I guess he likes young girls and maybe tried her and she fought him and he killed her."

"Before you heard about my husband, who'd you think killed her?"

Zelda sat back a little, and her eagerness faded some.

"What makes you think I'd have any idea?"

"You're a very bright and imaginative young woman. I'm sure the whole matter has been on your mind for weeks. That's perfectly natural. So what'd you decide?"

"Well, it seemed most likely, before now, that it must've been her brother Sven. I'd bet anything he hated Chris Kilbride, and figured he'd accused Gwendolen of carrying on with him, and maybe they fought and he lost his temper. He's very strong and could've done it, I bet."

"You ever talk with Sven?"

She shuddered and shook her head. "No. He's a spooky guy. I wouldn't dream of talking to him."

"Can you imagine who might've written the note to Chris Kilbride after Gwendolen was killed?"

She shrugged. "Maybe. I don't know."

"You ever talk any of all this over with Kate and Becky?"

"I never talked it over with anybody."

"That's hard for me to understand," said Hazel. "Any place I went to school and some awful thing happened, everybody talked it to death. Were classmates ashamed of not having liked Gwendolen—could that be why they didn't want to talk about her murder?"

"Maybe," said Zelda, and glanced at Hazel's wristwatch. "What time is it? I guess I should be getting home. I've got to do my chores."

At the door Zelda paused and looked back.

"Was any classmate of yours ever murdered?" she asked Hazel.

Hazel admitted none had been.

"That's what I figured," said Zelda, and left.

22

hat were you trying to get at?" I asked when Zelda was gone.

"Just fishing. I've a feeling she wrote the note to the Bible teacher, and I wouldn't be surprised if she wrote a note to Sven. Something asking him if he knew what his sister was up to. That make sense to you?"

I nodded. "But I can't quite figure Sven killing his sister, even by accident. The trouble is, I don't know enough about Gwendolen to figure just how she'd react if he jumped her about messing around with the Holy Roller."

"Well, I'll bet whatever the reaction was, it fell well short of being diplomatic."

The following day was Saturday, and I suggested that Hazel ride to Aquatown with me, and we'd drop in on Doc Severance and see what he could tell about his examination of Gwendolen after the killing. She agreed to go but said she'd do some shopping while I met with the doctor, since she suspected I'd get clearer answers without a woman in tow while asking questions about a dead girl's privates.

I don't imagine it gets much hotter in hell than South Dakota was late on a Saturday morning in August that year. We wheeled along with the windows wide open, except when we met other trucks or cars and had to roll up the windows to keep from being blinded by the gravel dust that made great clouds behind every moving vehicle. We'd had a good night—we hadn't done it that many times, but it was still a great tranquilizer. She sat in the seat, leaning into me lightly when the road was deserted, pulling a bit away when we passed through a small town or met other traffic. When you saw a car coming from a side road, you could see the dust trail behind it all the way to the horizon except when one of the stronger gusts of wind broke it up here and there.

I parked downtown in front of the biggest department store for Hazel's benefit, then walked a quarter of a block to the doctor's office, which was located over a drugstore. He was expecting me, as I'd made a call for an appointment. He hadn't sounded exactly enthusiastic but admitted he'd heard about my involvement in the Gwendolen case and said he would try to be helpful.

Doc Severance was short enough to look up to me and had gentle eyes, broad cheeks, and a narrow mouth with deep smile wrinkles framing it.

"The fact is," I told him, "I didn't quite have the gall to ask Dr. Westcott details about his daughter's condition when he examined her. What I want to know is, did he, or you, find any signs she'd been raped?"

"Did he say that was his diagnosis?"

Doc Severance's voice was gently husky.

"I got my report from the local cop, Driscoll."

"Well, I don't know what Dr. Westcott told the officer. I told him that the girl was not a virgin. I did not see evidence of violence, beyond the fractured arm and the evident bruises and damage to the throat. There were no bruises, cuts, or signs of abuse apparent on her lower body. I did find that there was semen in the vagina and made that clear to Officer Driscoll."

"Could that have happened after she was dead?"

"It is quite possible. Frankly, I've not had a lot of experience with that sort of examination. Actually, none at all."

"I get the feeling you don't think it was a rape."

"I'm telling you, I simply can't say one way or the other with certainty."

"Any idea how long she'd been dead when you saw her?"

"Probably over twelve hours. I saw her a bit before noon. It's likely she was killed somewhere between eight and midnight."

"Do you know Dr. Westcott well?"

"Not particularly. He has a good reputation, I know. A well-respected, thoroughly experienced professional."

"Was he there when you made your examination?"

"No. He'd gone home when I arrived after Officer Driscoll's request."

"Why do you think Driscoll wanted you to double-check Doc Westcott's examination?"

"I'd think that'd be quite obvious. Nothing could be more traumatic for a man than to examine the corpse of his own murdered daughter. You could hardly expect a coldly rational, scientific examination."

I agreed with him, offered my thanks for his time, and left.

I found Hazel in the grocery, where she had told me she'd most likely be, and tagged along as she finished her shopping. She was, I noticed, big on fruit and fresh vegetables.

She listened to my report and asked what I made of it.

"Not sure. Can't quite figure a guy killing a girl right after making out with her, but then I can't figure him killing her before either, although I've heard of ones who preferred the quiet partner. . . . Never been able to picture that."

"I'm glad. Now what?"

"Well, first there's this big sign to get finished. Then, if we haven't already had another visit from your loving hubby, maybe I'll snoop around trying to locate the bastard. What did you think of Zelda's notion that Derek did in Gwendolen?"

"It seems pretty unlikely. I mean, that he could just drift into town, catch her in the church basement, and do it. It's just too far-fetched that they'd even meet, let alone wind up in that place."

"You don't think, when you were Gwendolen's age, that Derek could have sweet-talked you into a little necking session?"

"It would depend. I guess we can't just assume, saying he did meet with her, that he hadn't run into her at some earlier time. But it still seems unlikely."

"Yeah, but wouldn't it be handy if we could wind up both cases in one neat package? Maybe we could frame him."

"That's a tempting idea. When you get the details worked out, let me know."

❦ 23 ❧

O n Monday I went around to talk with Officer Driscoll and brought up the possibility of Derek being the villain in Gwendolen's murder. It appealed to him. Just about any cop prefers to blame an outsider for crime in his territory. He even agreed to call cops in Sioux Falls to see if they could check if Derek was in town. All we got from that was a clear statement the man had not been in trouble with the law there in the past four years. That seemed to leave a lot of territory untouched, but it was evident our resources were not interested in ancient history, which took care of anything before the thirties.

After a lot of palaver, Driscoll let me call my old connection in Aquatown, who offered names of contacts in Yankton, Aberdeen, Milbank, Webster, and Brookings. Driscoll went along with the first two calls, but I had to pay for all the rest. Came up with sniffles. Finally called the Electrolux distributor in Sioux Falls and learned Derek hadn't been with them for over a year. No, said the guy I was talking to, he didn't know who Derek worked for now, but thought it might be some encyclopedia outfit.

I had worked most of Sunday on Pinkerton's sign, and Monday, after all the telephoning, I put on the finishing touches and thought about next steps. It seemed the best thing would be to make a sashay around a few neighboring towns, trying to find Hazel's slippery husband.

I was just getting cleaned up when Hazel came around. She had a worried look.

"What's wrong?" I asked.

"When I came back to the hotel from the library, Jud had a message for me. He said a man called, identified himself as Ted Harralson, and asked for me. When Jud told him where I was, he said he'd like to leave a message. 'Just tell her I called, and that I hope she hasn't forgotten me.' And then he hung up."

"Jud know if it was long distance?"

"He wasn't sure. It could have been, but he's not positive."

I pulled her close, and she grabbed me and hung on, pushing her face against mine.

I suggested we go eat, and she said she wasn't hungry but agreed to come along when I pushed, and eventually she managed to glance at the menu and order a hamburger.

"How come you never got a divorce?" I asked.

She sighed. "I suppose that would've been the sensible thing to do. But after the first mad-on, I just didn't want to get involved with a lawyer and all the mess of trying to prove he'd been making love to a kid in my own living room, and worrying about paying a lawyer. And there was the fact that Derek can be about the best liar I ever met and would take real pleasure in making me out as the one at fault. He'd countersue, and with his tricky cleverness and smooth tongue, it'd be a nightmare. Later on, when I thought about it, I realized having run off put me in the position of being the deserter, and it just seemed too much."

"What if you wanted to get married to someone else?"

"Well," she said, giving me a thoughtful look, "I suppose that won't happen until I find a guy who can untangle it all for me."

"That shouldn't be too hard for you to manage."

"We'll see, won't we?"

"Yeah. Maybe we ought to go back to the hotel and think about it some more."

"All right. But if we go to bed I doubt we'll think much."

"When I've got you in bed, I think all the time. It's kind of in one general direction, I'll admit, but I really work at it."

"I believe it. You've got great talent in that line. Just for appearance sake, I'll leave here first, okay?"

"No, we'll go together. Then you can go up to the room and I'll join you in a few minutes."

"Do you want me to get a divorce?"

"Yeah. But I don't think we can handle that tonight."

She spread her arms in mock hopelessness, and we both got up to leave.

When Hazel had gone up to her room, I drifted to the kitchen and found Purita sitting at the table by a window, listening to a radio and knitting something brown.

"Hope you don't mind," I said, "got another question."

"Want a cup of coffee?"

"Why not?"

She filled a cup as I sat on the chair opposite hers, put it down beside me, took her seat, and shoved the knitting to one side as she took me in.

"I wondered," I said, "if you know which town Dora Lynne's friend May Banks moved to in California."

"Eureka."

"How'd you happen to know?"

A big smile did wonders for her face, making the chin less aggressive and showing perfect white teeth.

"May sends Christmas cards," she said. "Even sends them to Jud. You know what the town name means?"

"Tell me."

"I have found it. That's what the Greek man who learned how to test gold said. 'Eureka! I have found it.' In the note with her first card to me, she said it was a perfect name because California and that town was like finding gold to her."

"Can you give me her phone number?"

"*Sí. You wait.*"

She got up, went up the nearby stairs to her room, and returned a moment later with the number written down on a torn slip of paper.

"What will you ask her?"

"Whatever she can tell me about Derek."

She raised her heavy eyebrows. "That might become an expensive call."

"She know him that well?"

"She doesn't have to know a thing to talk a lot."

≪ 24 ≫

ack in the lobby I called the number Purita had given me and got a busy signal. Thinking of Purita's warning about how long a chat with May could be, it seemed wise to go tell Hazel what I was working on. She told me, a little too kindly, that she could probably wait awhile.

"Okay if I have to wake you when I come up?"

She grinned. "I'd prefer it that way. Wouldn't want to miss out on anything."

I headed back down to the telephone, intent on making the call brief.

May answered on the first ring.

"Purita, here at the Pickett Hotel, tells me you were a good friend of Dora Lynne, is that right?"

"Of course—who are you?"

I told her, with emphasis on being hired by Pastor Bjornson, and gave her a quickie on my assignment.

"What's a murder of—who was it? Gwendolen?—got to do with Dora Lynne?"

"Dora's disappeared. She's been gone from her shop over a

day, and her parents say she's with a guy we suspect is Derek Warford. We're anxious because Warford might have been Gwendolen's killer."

"That's ridiculous. Derek's a lover, not a killer. Besides, I happen to know he just married Dora."

"When?"

"A day or so ago. That's why she left Jonesville. He swept her away."

"You've talked with her?"

"Of course, how else would I know? She called to tell me she was going to—she was so excited she could barely talk."

"Was it a surprise?"

"I was about struck dumb. I mean, Derek's good looking and smooth enough to get just about any girl, and he sure tries for them all."

"Including you?"

"Why not? I'm not that bad. To tell you the truth, he'd probably have tried even Purita if he'd met her. Derek's every lady's man, or wants to be. And he's cute enough to get away with it. Lord, what a line!"

"If that's the case, I'd think you'd be surprised he asked anybody to marry him, especially Dora."

"You say that like you'd met her."

"No, but I saw her. There's nothing wrong with her, but she didn't seem flashy enough for a guy like Warford."

"Well, sometime his type surprises you. I mean, they get the gate from some gorgeous doll and decide what they want is a girl who really needs and appreciates them."

"The trouble is, this guy's already married. You ever hear of Hazel Warford?"

"I don't think so. Who's she?"

"Derek's wife. She was married to him a few years back and

dumped him when she caught him with their fourteen-year-old housekeeper. She came to Jonesville a couple years ago and has been around ever since."

"Didn't she divorce him?"

"No. Just took off. About a year later, a guy she'd been dating got killed in a hit-and-run, and Derek called her the week after and hinted he'd done it. He also trashed her apartment a couple times. After the second time she took off without leaving a forwarding address and landed here."

"Why're you telling me this?"

"Because I think your friend is in trouble, and I hope if she gets in touch, you'll fill her in on this bird's act. If you can't convince her to shake him, at least find out where she is and let me know, so we can keep him from doing anything to her."

"Oh, God. I suppose I should. . . . She promised to keep in touch. We were really quite good friends; she's a good kid."

No, she didn't know where the supposed marriage took place; in fact she wasn't certain it had happened yet at the time of their talk. I worked hard on her, trying to make her see it was important for me to catch up with this dude, and she seemed convinced by the time we hung up.

Hazel was wide awake when I entered her room. We didn't talk much about May. After the first round, which you might class as a double knockout, we came to for a while and discussed the call in more detail. She didn't think May would hear from Dora again.

We dropped that and started talking about our own future. She allowed as how she wouldn't necessarily have to move to a big city to get her life organized if she had a better offer.

"You only do your sign-painting business summers, don't you?" she asked.

"Sometimes I start May and run into September."

"What do you do the rest of the year?"

"Well, pretty often I've helped run my old man's hotel in Corden. I can probably do that anytime I want. The old man can't handle it alone anymore."

"I don't think you should call him your old man. It's not respectful, it's denigrating."

"It's no worse than him calling me Hey You. When he talks about me to anybody else, I'm his hobo kid."

"Well, you both should grow up. If I got a job teaching in Corden, we could do all right. Or would it cramp your style if I traveled with you summers?"

"I think it would considerably class up my act. Are you starting to think about a divorce from Derek, every girl's dream boy?"

"If you can get him convicted of any of his crimes, it ought to be relatively easy for me to get a divorce. Then you could make an honest woman of me."

"I guess I'd do anything to make you—an honest woman, that is."

"You just guess?"

I sighed and said I was afraid so and she gave me a punch, which led to a bit of wrestling, and then we were suddenly at it again and even after we were all through, it was plain as exhaustion that living with this woman was the most important thing on my horizon.

I told her so and she said something that sounded like Thank God and, when I pressed her, said she was very happy because if she had to make love to me again this night to convince me of that need, she might not survive for marriage later.

When I was beginning to doze off, she asked what would happen if I became responsible for the hotel completely.

"I'd dump it."

"Why?"

"There's no business for small-town hotels anymore. Salesmen park in the big towns, hit the bigger markets, don't want to go down the hall to the can. The only thing that keeps us in business now is the money from apartment rentals. Elihu has been adding a new apartment on the average of every other year. And the way things are going in Corden, there probably won't be a hell of a lot of folks needing apartments around there before long. The town's shrinking—anybody who can manage heads for California, the poorer ones try for Minneapolis, the desperate go to Aquatown or Sioux Falls. Our farmers are damned near starving, but they still manage to grow some food; you can figure how tough it is for small-town folks."

"You make any money solving murders?"

"Barely expenses—and it's a long time between them in this territory."

"Well, you'd better think all this over before you get carried away about us getting together. If one of those rubbers fails us, I sure won't get an abortion. And I'd rather not raise a kid alone."

"You think you might have a girl?"

"My mother did, I don't know why I can't. What've you got against boys?"

"Well, I've got two nephews. Seems like there ought to be a girl in my generation."

"I guess you're thinking about the little girl that adopted you, huh?"

"Yeah."

"Well, if it happens, should we name her Alma?"

"I'd like that."

"Carl, you're a sentimental bum. I love you. Go to sleep."

arly Tuesday morning I drifted around to the Westcott house and found Sven mowing the lawn, the only one on the block well enough watered to need a trim. As I turned in at their walk, he pulled up and frowned at me.

"Now what?" he asked.

"You look like a man needs a break. Can we talk a minute?"

"About what?"

"You remember a guy named Derek Warford?"

He shook his head.

"He peddled vacuum cleaners around here some years back. Good-lookin' dude, liked to talk to anybody, including kids. What kind of a cleaner have you got here?"

"Electrolux."

"How long you had it?"

"I dunno. Quite a while. You'd have to ask Ma."

So I went and knocked on the door while the dutiful son went back to mowing.

Martha answered the door so quickly it seemed likely she'd heard me talking to her son and was hovering in the hall. She

greeted me politely and invited me in. Yes, she remembered buy-
ing the machine. It was five years ago. The salesman had been
very persuasive, and she was impressed by the machine at once.
She'd even given the man coffee and they talked about the children, who seemed to interest him a great deal. No, she didn't
remember his name until I offered it and immediately smiled and
said yes, that was familiar. Derek. The last name meant nothing.

"He talk to Sven and Gwendolen?"

"No, Sven was off somewhere, as usual. But Gwendolen was
home and he certainly talked to her. He made a big fuss over her,
and she loved it."

"Ever seen him since?"

"No. But he sent a couple postcards. Addressed them to
Gwendolen. She was thrilled to death."

"Nothing lately?"

"Not that I know of."

"Who looks at the mail first here?"

Her mouth drooped. "Gwendolen almost always picked it
up. She got letters from a couple teachers, and Chris dropped her
notes now and then."

"Did she save letters?"

"I assumed she did, but we found none in her room after—"

"Could I see the room?"

"Oh, well, I guess so. Why not?"

We went up a straight flight of stairs, did a U-turn at the top,
and walked along a short hall to the door at its end. It was open,
and Martha led the way inside. It had the neatness of a guest
room, all surfaces clear of clutter except a nightstand beside the
bed where a small stack of books stood next to a yellow-shaded
lamp with a white base designed like a Roman column. I saw *Age
of Reason*, Conrad's *Lord Jim* and *The Rover*, and *Two Little Sav-
ages*, by Ernest Thompson Seton.

"Didn't she read any girls' books?" I asked.

"When she was little, yes. Nancy Drew and some others, but last year she decided they were all silly and gave them away. These were ones she got for Christmas."

"Who gave her the Seton book?"

She smiled for the first time. "Sven. I think he felt it might make her understand boys better. That was nearly four years ago."

"Did it help?"

"I'm afraid not. Frankly, I'm surprised she kept it."

It made me like Gwendolen better. She had at least that much sentimentality. Religious pictures dominated the walls, including ones I seemed to have seen a dozen times. Mostly Jesus was alone and in deep thought—as though already anticipating the cross. He has always struck me as the loneliest soul ever pictured.

I opened drawers in the desk, half expecting an objection from Martha, but she only looked on and told me she had gone through everything and found no diaries, letters, or notes.

"But she saved favorite books."

"Yes, that's true. There are more in the closet."

I looked in and was surprised to find no clothes on hangers or hooks.

"The doctor donated all of Gwendolen's clothing to Pastor Bjornson's church," she said before I could ask. "For distribution to the needy."

It was plain from her tone this had not been a mutual decision.

Books were stacked on the floor, and I recognized only *Little Women*, which was on top of one stack. There was nothing else to look at, so I moved back into the bedroom.

Gwendolen had liked sunshiny colors—yellow, orange,

pink, and combinations of them with shades of green. The only souvenir of childhood in sight was a stuffed rabbit on the bed between the pillows. It was missing the left ear.

"Did you ever see her writing in a diary?"

"No, but I know she had one, at least. She left it out once or twice. I didn't look at it—it wouldn't be right."

That was a little too defensive sounding to convince me, but I let it ride. She seemed too vulnerable to push. At the same time I rejected the notion of asking whether Sven ever came into his sister's room. It wouldn't really mean anything if she knew or not.

"You strip the bed after Gwendolen died?" I asked.

She blinked and looked that way. "No. Her father did that. Then he made it up fresh and left it the way it is now. He'd never made a bed before since we were married. Maybe never."

She gave me an apologetic smile. "Doctors don't have time for doing housework."

"Did he have much time for his children?"

She didn't quite flinch, but the probe bothered her.

"I'm afraid not. And that's another reason he's so badly hurt by what happened. The missed chances, you know? I mean, of getting to really know her. He doesn't talk about it, but I can tell. . . ."

"Did you know her well?"

She took a deep breath and slowly shook her head.

"I thought so when she was a little girl. Although very early on it was plain she was brighter than most children and—I don't know—difficult to reach. By the time she was thirteen she was reading all the time and talking only to teachers, and then that Bible man. She didn't have time for her mother. She seemed to look down on me. Was very impatient—no—I'm not being fair. It was difficult for her to deal with people who didn't understand the things she was so fascinated by—the books—foreign countries and people. She had such a busy mind—"

"Have you seen the man lately who sold you the vacuum cleaner five years back?"

"No. Why do you ask that?"

"He's been around. I just wondered if it was possible he'd seen Gwendolen."

She stared at me. "You think maybe he—?"

"According to what I've heard, this guy had a weakness for young girls. It's just something I'd like to check out."

She sat down on the edge of the couch and watched me, wide-eyed.

"I can't imagine—he was such a nice man—so handsome." She blushed, and shook her head. "I guess that doesn't mean anything, does it? That he was nice, I mean. But how—?"

"He might have written to her, made an appointment, for all we know. A guy like that would be pretty irresistible to any girl so young, no matter how smart."

She said "Oh Lord," and began to cry.

26

azel was into her period that night, so we only talked. She tried again to convince me that Derek wasn't a killer. My argument was that she stretched coincidence clear out of joint if she thought her ex-boyfriend was only accidentally killed in the hit-and-run, and then some stranger just happened to run me off the road in a stolen truck.

"Well, it's quite a different thing for a man to kill a couple men who were trying to take his wife than for him to strangle a girl in a church basement."

"Yeah. It'd be easier to kill the girl."

"That's not my point."

"You know what? Maybe we shouldn't talk when we can't make love. We both get owly."

"I'm not owly, I'm just being logical."

"How about if I just kiss you?"

She thought about that a few seconds before allowing as how she could tolerate that pretty well. A while later we went to sleep.

In the morning I had a call from Captain Baker, in Aquatown.

"I think we got a line on your boy Derek," he said.

"Tell me."

"I had one of my guys, Lassiter, check with the local vacuum cleaner place—Electrolux? Yeah. He found out your boy's into encyclopedias. He talked with a manager who was buddies with Warford. And you're never gonna guess where he's been operating lately."

"So why don't you just tell me?"

"In your little old hometown, Corden."

I thanked him and said I'd follow that up.

Hazel was in the school library when I walked in, and she arched her eyebrows at me.

"Looking for something to read?" she asked.

"Can you take a couple days off?"

"Well, I'm pretty overwhelmed with duties, but maybe I could slip out for a while and not get fired, since this is a volunteer job summers. We going to Paris?"

"If you're really interested, we could hit Corden for a quickie. Visit, that is, considering your condition."

"How come?"

I told her of Baker's call. Her eyes widened. "Maybe you'd better call your folks and make sure he's not staying at their hotel."

"Already checked. Nobody like Derek's signed in. He's probably staying at a hotel in Aquatown and moving out from there. But it won't hurt if we drop by and check around town a little. You can meet Elihu and Ma."

"When do we go?"

"Well, first I've got to get the sign put up over the door of Pinkerton's Pavilion and collect my pay. Meanwhile you get clear and pack a nightie. Then we're off."

When we finally went, the wind was blowing fierce enough to raise dust that turned the sky hazy. The temperature was in the upper nineties. We rattled along the graveled road, adding our share of pollution and not talking much because of the racket. Hazel was wearing a deep blue dress with short sleeves and a low collar. She had offered to wear glasses—a pose she'd assumed when she applied for her job at the school—but I voted against it, saying if she couldn't get by on her natural talents, better she should flunk, because people in my family had eagle eyes for phonies, and besides, she already looked too smart.

"You mean to get mixed up with you?"

"Are you mixed up?"

She leaned into me and said, "No, I'm involved. And I won't admit that's not smart to anybody but you. How much of this state have you covered? I mean, as a sign painter?"

"Most of the east-central part."

"How do you choose where you'll go?"

"Well, most of the time I pick towns between a thousand and fifteen hundred people. That's where it's not likely there'll be a local sign painter. There's something near thirty towns that size."

"Which are your favorites?"

"They're pretty much alike. I've always favored Corden, but that's probably because I know it best. Fact is, though, it has more trees than average in this state, and it's on a sort of hillside so it's not as monotonous as places just parked on flat prairie."

"Any pet names?"

"Yeah, but they're not for towns I've hit. One's named Letcher, the other Woonsocket. They're pretty close together, somewhere between Huron and Mitchell, but somehow I've never worked in either of them."

We approached Corden from the west so she couldn't see it until we came over the rolling prairie, which suddenly dipped and we were wheeling along the graveled highway that sloped down into town.

It was only about four city blocks before we reached the hotel on the south side of the street. There were elms lining the highway on both sides and shading the collection of small and medium-sized houses, mostly white, many in need of paint. If you looked close you could see paved sidewalks in need of repair much of the way. In the business section, which ran for two blocks, east and west, and one block north, there were half a dozen cars angle-parked at the high curbs, mostly Chevies and Fords, with one Buick for variety. I swung around the corner where the Wilcox Hotel stood, and parked opposite the front door.

Hazel got out slowly and squinted at the hotel sign bolted along the front of the balcony over the front door.

"I suppose you painted that," she said.

"Matter of fact, it was done by my teacher, Larry. I added a fresh coat of paint a couple years back."

"You don't seem to have spoiled it any."

I could see Elihu through the window to the left of the front door. He was laboriously trying to get on his feet. We went up to the door, I pulled open the screen, Hazel stepped inside, and I followed.

Elihu grinned like an ape ready for feed as I made the introductions, and accepted Hazel's hand with both of his. He said he was proud to meet her. She said likewise and put her right hand on his upper arm for a second. His grin got even broader, then he ducked his head, let her go, and turned his head to holler, "Min!"

Ma came in through the door to the alcove they called the office, and the next moment had joined us. She gave Hazel her special once-over, smiled politely, and suggested we go to the dining room, since Bertha had lunch ready to serve.

The dining room had been closed to the public a few years before but still had all of its tables and the booths, since Elihu hadn't been up to converting it all to another apartment or two as yet. A couple mild heart attacks had slowed him down considerably.

I had filled Ma in on Hazel's background over the telephone, with special stress on the seriousness of her problem with her husband. I knew her well enough to figure she'd reserve judgment until they'd actually talked, at the same time knowing she would take any tales from me with a full shaker of salt.

We sat at the round table a few steps from the swinging kitchen doors and were served by a maid new to me, a stocky girl in her late teens with fairly short brown hair and pale eyebrows over dark blue eyes with long lashes. She never looked at me directly, as though she'd had warnings about the wolf in bum's clothing and was being careful to avoid notice.

Bertha had prepared bean soup, which was hot, well spiced, and satisfying.

Hazel, with my encouragement, gave Elihu and Ma the full picture regarding Derek.

"What kinda car's he got?" asked Elihu.

"He favors Oldsmobiles," said Hazel, "but I don't really know what he has now. His cars are usually quite new and very well polished."

That was about enough to convince Elihu the guy couldn't be all bad. He had loved the Olds he owned before his current Dodge, which he felt was a comedown. He also respected a man who kept his car looking new.

Ma wasn't so warped. Just hearing the guy had made the maid and vandalized Hazel's apartment was enough to convince her he rated the noose.

"You want to see Joey Paxton," she told me. "He'll be here in a little while. I've asked him to come around."

Joey looked no different from any other time except when

he'd had pneumonia: still tall, gangling, and near apologetic. He examined Hazel with brief glances and approving smiles and turned sad when she filled him in on details about our target.

Yes, he figured he'd probably seen the man briefly a couple times. Once at a citizen's door, another time at the local café."

"Anybody with him?" I asked.

"Only at the café. Quiet-looking young lady."

That was a relief. I was half afraid he might have done her in.

The sightings had been a couple days back. No, he didn't know what kind of car the guy had—hadn't seen him in it, but thought he remembered noticing an out-of-town Olds at the curb in front of the café.

I asked whose house he'd seen the man at. He said it belonged to the Nelsons—Wes, the lawyer and landholder, and his wife, Carole—and we went over to check. That is, Joey and I went. Hazel stayed at the hotel and was talking with Elihu and Ma in the lobby when we left.

It was a short ways, so we walked. Joey told me that Hazel didn't look like a woman who would have been married to a man like the one he'd been hearing about.

"Well," I said, "whoring killers don't always wear a sign on their foreheads warning you off."

Joey looked a little pained but didn't go on about it.

The house was one of Corden's larger and better-kept homes on the generally better-kept south side of town. We went up three steps to a broad porch with a freshly painted glider to the right, and Joey tapped on the screen door edge.

A handsome, brown-haired woman showed up, smiled at him, and glanced at me with the kind of curious look I usually get at first meetings. Joey introduced her as Mrs. Nelson, and me as Carl Wilcox. Her eyes gave me a second look, which told me the name was familiar to her.

"We're trying to check up on a salesman who was around this last week," said Joey. "Happened to see him at your door, and wondered if you could tell us anything about him?"

"That would have been Friday, wouldn't it?" she said. "Yes, his name was Derek. That was the first name—I don't remember he mentioned his last. He was selling encyclopedias. Is something wrong?"

"We're just trying to locate him now. Did he give you an address where you could get hold of him?"

"Well now, he left some papers, I'll have to look. You want to come in?"

We followed her into the hall, took a left, and were in a comfortable living room with a vaguely patterned deep brown rug and plush-covered couch, an easy chair in light brown, and a whopping leather-covered easy chair with a footstool, no doubt for the man of the house. There were also side tables with fat lamps and broad shades, scattered about where they'd do the most good. A fat white Angora looked at us warily from the plush-covered chair, and its fluffy tail twitched slowly. We parked on the couch, and a moment later the lady was back with some papers that told us the encyclopedia company was out of New York. There was no local address for the rep.

"As I remember, he said he was just passing through on his way to Aquatown, then Minneapolis, but as he drove by, he saw our house and thought we were just the sort of people who'd want a set of encyclopedias, so he stopped to try us. He is a very charming man."

"So we hear," said Joey, with his most reassuring nod.

"Did you buy a set of encyclopedias?" I asked.

"Yes," she said, looking at me sharply. "Why, is there something wrong?"

"We don't know for sure," said Joey in his soothing tone. "It's kind of complicated. Did you notice if there was a woman out in his car?"

"Not until he left. I looked out when he drove away and thought I saw a woman's head on the right side, but wasn't really sure. Why do you ask?"

"Part of our problem is trying to locate a woman who might be with him," I said. "Did you happen to notice what kind of car he came in?"

No, she hadn't. That wasn't the sort of thing she paid a lot of attention to. She was fairly certain it was black, and that it wasn't cheap or very old. She was quite sure of that. No, she'd not seen his license plate.

"I think you should tell me what this is all about. I gave him a check, do you think I'll get the books? I should know what to expect—"

"The problem's not with him cheating customers," Joey assured her. "We've no record of that. In fact, we're not real sure he's done anything wrong. But he's been separated from his wife a few years and she claims he's been hounding her and there have been a couple accidents with guys she's been close to lately that look fishy. We're just trying to check it out."

She looked at me. "Have you had an accident?"

I couldn't help but grin. "Yeah, I did. Somebody ran me off a road with a truck. Wrecked my car. But we don't know it was Derek."

"I take it you know his wife."

"Less than a week."

"Well," she said, "you're not usually involved much longer than that anyway, are you?"

That took care of my grin, which was what she was after.

Before I could crack back, Joey asked her to let him know if she heard anything further from Derek, or if she had any trouble getting her encyclopedias delivered.

She assured him that he'd be the first to know.

When we were outside, I suggested we check with the neighbors to see if Derek had tried any of them. He agreed.

Neither of the neighboring homes was as classy as the Nelsons', but they weren't shacks either. No one was at home in the first one. In the second, a crotchety old man named Anson said no salesman had been around he could remember. Joey conceded, as we walked on, that it wasn't out of the question Anson wouldn't remember if the man had been there half an hour before.

No one else on either side of the block had seen or heard of Derek Warford.

"Well," said Joey, "I guess he's not always a liar. He must have picked the Nelson house because he figured there was money there."

"Either that," I said, "or he saw Mrs. Nelson around the place. But come to think of it, he'd probably only be interested if she had a teenage daughter."

"Well, actually she does. Ermine. She's fourteen or fifteen."

I talked him into telephoning Mrs. Nelson to ask if her daughter had been present when the salesman called. She told him she'd been on the front porch when he arrived, and she brought him in. Yes, she'd stayed for the pitch and had been very strongly in favor of the purchase. Joey asked if the daughter and the salesman had been alone together at any time. I was proud of him, but the answer was no, or at least not after he first came up on the porch and started talking to her. And no, Mrs. Nelson was certain he had not been back in touch with her daughter. If she heard anything new, she would let Joey know.

27

ack at the hotel I found Elihu playing solitaire at the salesmen's table in the lobby. He told me Hazel was in the parlor
with Ma.

I asked him how he was doing.

"Well, I won one and lost two, so far."

"Did you cheat?"

"If I cheated I'd win 'em all. Or most."

"Actually, I was asking how's the heart."

He scowled at me suspiciously. "Why? You want to come
back and take over the place?"

"What the hell makes you think I'd want this headache?"

"Can't think of any other reason you'd be asking after my
health."

"Pure nosiness, Elihu. It's a habit I've picked up messing with
killers and crooks. How do you like Hazel?"

"She's all right. Maybe better. But got damned poor taste in
men."

"Oh, did she take to you?"

"She came with you, that's how I know. How in the pluper-fect hell did you manage to get next to her?"

"Because she's married to a guy who's been giving her trouble, and may have killed a guy she dated."

"Well, you'd think that'd make her more careful about who she goes riding around the country with."

I gave him up and went into the parlor. Ma was sitting on the couch with Hazel on her right, showing her samples of tatting she'd done. It was all cozy as a drawing by the guy who does *Saturday Evening Post* covers. Hazel gave me a welcoming grin, while Ma just kept explaining her techniques with tatting needles. When she ran down, she lifted her head and acknowledged me, grudgingly.

"How well do you know the Nelsons?" I asked.

"They're Catholics," she said, as though that covered the subject.

"What's their daughter like?"

"Well, I can't say I know much about her. She's pretty enough, I suppose. Rather fancies herself, from what I hear. Her mother's pushy. They're rather well off, and like to let everybody know it."

"How old is the daughter?" asked Hazel.

"Oh, she's one of those fourteen-going-on-twenty types. Why do you ask?"

"Because Hazel's husband had a weakness for girls around that age and we think he may have tried promoting something. Hazel, we've got to find some way of getting you to talk to this girl. Find out if Derek's made any follow-up."

She looked a little pained, but nodded in agreement.

I looked at Ma and asked, "You know any teachers at the high school we could ask about students in her class?"

She didn't, but said she'd ask The Girl about it. The Girl

was what Ma always called any maid who worked in the hotel.

I asked for the name, and she said it was Pearl.

Pearl stood stiffly in the middle of the parlor while Ma explained to her what I was about and, when I invited her to sit down, parked at the edge of a padded chair near the double French doors leading to Ma's bedroom.

Yes, she knew the Nelson daughter by sight but little more. She said she had been in Miss Hendrickson's class. Miss Hendrickson was a crippled teacher who lived on the west hill near the edge of town.

The teacher had no telephone, so Hazel and I walked up for a visit. We were greeted promptly at the door by a birdlike woman with a sharp beak, and hawk eyes that had no doubt dominated many a classroom of juveniles. Her hair was thin and prematurely gray. Pearl had said she was in her early forties, but she looked well into her sixties. By mutual agreement, Hazel explained our mission while I sat by and took it all in.

"We've no reason to believe anything out of line has happened," Hazel began. "What we're looking for is background information that might help us figure out what a man named Derek Warford might be up to. He's my husband—we've been separated for a couple of years—" She went on to cover the cause of the breakup, the harassment since, and the suspicion of murder in the case of a suitor of hers and the attempt on my life.

"Where do I come in?" demanded Miss Hendrickson.

"We understand you had a girl named Ermine Nelson in your class this past session?"

"Yes, I did."

"What can you tell us about her?"

"She's rather attractive, has a fairly good mind and a hyperactive imagination. A very social sort of girl. Will no doubt be a society leader one day."

"Many close friends?"

"Oh yes indeed. Why're you asking?"

Hazel looked at me.

"We think this Derek guy might have made a play for her. He's had a record of going after younger girls. We know he was in the home of the Nelsons selling encyclopedias a couple days ago, and that the girl was out on the front porch when he passed the house, so we guess he stopped as much because of her as because it was a fancy home and they'd have money. He hadn't tried his pitch to any of the close neighbors. Ermine's mother doesn't think Derek's been in touch since that first call at their house, but from what we know of this guy, we figure if he hasn't got to her yet, he soon will. We wonder if you know how easy she might be?"

"If the fellow's good looking and well dressed, I imagine she encouraged his flirting. I think she's vamped half the males in her class, and she still manages to be popular with the girls."

We talked some more, getting a few names of Ermine's classmates, and finally I thanked her and went back to the hotel. A young girl was sitting in the rocker immediately opposite the front door as we entered, and I guessed at once it had to be Ermine. She was slender, with a perfect complexion, large gray eyes, and soft brown hair framing a sprightly face. Ma was sitting to her left, and Elihu, as usual, was parked in his swivel chair by the front window next to the door.

"You have a visitor," Ma said.

"Ermine Nelson?" I asked.

The girl flashed her smile, which brought dimples and was about enough to make any boy her age dizzy.

"Mother said you wanted to talk with me."

"Right. Let's go into the dining room, where we won't get interrupted."

That made no hit with the elders, but only Elihu growled. Ma gave him her What-could-you-expect? look.

"So what can you tell us?" I asked as Hazel and I sat in a booth across from Ermine.

"What do you want to know?"

"Have you heard from Derek since he came to your house and sold the encyclopedias?"

"No."

"When he approached you at the house, did the two of you talk any before you took him in to your mother?"

"Oh yes," she said, smiling brightly. "He told me I was prettier than a bouquet of roses and asked if I was a college student yet, and I said no, I was a bit young for that, and he said I looked smart and grown-up enough to be whatever I wanted, and I said he looked more like a movie actor than a traveling salesman, which I supposed he was, and he said that was the nicest compliment he'd had all morning, maybe all week, and he sort of perched on the porch railing and just smiled at me until I asked what he was selling. You know what he said? He said he was selling opportunities. A chance to enrich my life, learn about the world, and set high goals. And then Mother came to the door and asked what he wanted."

"I guess you were disappointed."

"Was I ever," she admitted.

"Did you take in the whole sales pitch?"

"Oh sure. Wouldn't have missed it for anything. He showed us pictures in the books—it's an illustrated set, Compton's, just beautiful."

"Did he pay you a lot of attention all through his pitch?"

"Oh," she dimpled again, "he was very careful to make it look like he was concentrating on my mom, but he managed all along to include me as he talked, and his smile was different when he looked at me than when he looked at her. I mean, his eyes would sort of glow, you know? Mom was so impressed by the books I didn't think she noticed at the time, but I guess she did. She's real sharp."

"But Derek didn't have any chance to ask anything about you, like information about places you visit, cafés or soda fountains—"

She shook her head.

"No personal questions about either you or your mother?"

"He just asked did we read much and wouldn't it be fun to know stuff other people didn't, or to be able to look up stuff we wondered about."

"You heard from him or seen him since that day?"

"No," she said, looking me straight in the eye.

"Okay. What'd your mother tell you about us?"

"She said you work with the police and think maybe Derek killed someone and might try to get me alone."

"If he does get in touch, will you let us know?"

"What'll you do to him?"

"Well," said Hazel, "our first concern is to keep him from taking advantage of you. But the police want to ask him questions about where he was when my friend was killed by a hit-and-run driver, and also where he was when Carl here was run off a road by a truck a couple days ago."

"Why's Derek a suspect?"

"Because we know he tries to bed young girls—I caught him with one on the couch in our living room some years ago, so I know this is a fact. Because he has vandalized apartments I lived in and called me to make threats against any man I might show an interest in. He's dangerous. I think he's more than just jealous, he's crazy. Okay?"

Ermine took all of this in soberly, and near the end she was frowning. She shook her head slowly.

"That's doesn't sound like the man we heard talking. Not a bit. He was all fun."

"Oh sure," said Hazel, "that's his specialty. Being fun. I know. I did marry him, after all. That way you get to know all sides of a man."

"Will you let us know if you hear from him?" I asked.

Ermine nodded, almost absently, then looked me in the eye again and said, "Yes. I will."

After she was gone I asked Hazel if she believed her.

"No, and it's my fault. I was stupid. Let my emotions take over. She didn't believe me at all. She probably has the notion I'm a scorned woman, after revenge. If Derek does make an approach, she'll agree to meet him so she can hear his side. And I can guess how that'd go. Derek's big on making a case for himself."

"If you were in her place, is that the way you'd have played it at her age?"

"Oh Lord," she sighed, "I'm afraid so."

Plainly he'd be more convincing talking to a young woman in a café or park, face-to-face, than lying to a character like me through a tent canvas in the dark. The problem was, you can't put surveillance on a young woman in a town the size of Corden and not have it obvious as clown makeup. The only thing in our favor was, it wouldn't be easy for him to make an approach in this burg without being spotted.

I decided we'd better get back to Corden's cop, Joey Paxton.

28

oey, in his office at City Hall, took in my report on our talks with the Nelson women while slouched in his chair and twiddling his thumbs.

"It might be a good idea," I suggested, "if you talked with Mrs. Nelson and got it across to her she should make damned sure her Ermine doesn't get cozy with this dude. Hazel pretty much laid out to the kid what kind of a bastard Derek is, but she got carried away and suspects all she did was make her defensive for the peddler. How about Ermine's father? Shouldn't we have a talk with him?"

He considered that, sighed, sat forward, leaned both elbows on his desk, and said yeah, but not the three of us. Just him and me. Hazel was wise enough to let the snub go by, said she'd talk some more with my mother.

Nelson's law office was upstairs over the bank. We went in a side door and up the stairs on the east side of the building. It was a one-room office, wide and deep, with the secretary's desk just inside the door and the man himself well off in the back behind a large, well-polished desk. The secretary was a woman of many years, with gray hair and a round face that resisted wrinkles except around the eyes and the corners of her wide mouth. She smiled at Joey after her first surprised glance when we walked in, and gave me a brief examination before asking what she could do for us.

"Like to have a few minutes with your boss," said Joey, concentrating on her as though he couldn't acknowledge Nelson's presence until his secretary gave her permission.

Nelson got up, moved around his desk, and approached with his hand extended.

"Come on in, Joey. And hello, Carl, it's been a while."

He shook hands with both of us, and we went back to his space, took the chairs he pulled from beside the wall, and parked facing him.

I had never met him formally, just seen him around town a few times and fairly often having lunch with friends or clients in the Wilcox Hotel café when it was a favorite dining spot a few years back. He was the big-personality type, a tall, solid man with smooth pink skin, carefully brushed hair, a crinkly grin, and a voice like John Barrymore's, rich and convincing.

"So," he asked me when we were settled, "what brings you back to town in August?"

"Murder," I said.

"Really? Well then, I guess some villain is in big trouble, right? Where do I come in?"

I glanced at Joey, who just nodded, and went into my story about Gwendolen, working on around to Derek Warford. The name Derek rang a bell. He said of course, the encyclopedia man, the women's delight.

"Ever see him?"

"No, but I heard more about him than seemed necessary. What's the point of this? What's he done?"

"We think, since Derek's got a record of messing around with real young girls, he might try getting cozy with your Ermine. Derek's wife, who walked out on him two years ago because she caught him doing a fourteen-year-old in her parlor, was with me when I talked with your daughter. We're afraid our warning only made her suspicious that Derek's being attacked because his wife is still sore at him and wants to get him in big trouble. We both figure your daughter's a real bright kid, but Derek's a smooth article and might manage to convince her he's been the wronged one—I've already had his story about his wife being the one who fooled around, and know exactly the line he uses. We've come here because we hope that you can convince her, first, that she shouldn't let this guy within yelling distance, and second, if he does get in touch, that she try to find out where he is so we can land him."

"What evidence do you have that he killed this girl in Jonesville?"

"Not a smidgen. But we know his weakness for young girls, we've been tipped off by the Aquatown police that he's been working this territory, and we know he met her a few years back and left a big impression on her."

"All right. I'll talk with Ermine tonight."

Joey leaned forward.

"Wes, just between us guys, you think you can reach her?"

For a second I thought he was going to get mad, then he lowered his head a notch. When he raised it once more he was smiling.

"That's a pretty embarrassing question, Joey. I'm not at all sure I can answer it honestly. She always appears to listen, but all too often I'm not sure she hears. If you'd ever had a daughter, you might understand what I'm saying. With a girl like Ermine, you never have confrontations or genuine arguments. She takes suggestions, weighs them, and pretty much goes her own way. But she's smart enough never to let it be obvious. If she could make Derek talk with her on the telephone long enough to get the answers she wants, she'd do it. I doubt very much she'd let him lure her into any private place where he could have his way with her. And finally, it's blamed unlikely, in any event, that she would set him up to be caught, since she liked him so well when they met. I can only try."

When we were back on the street I asked Joey how good a lawyer he thought Nelson was.

"Well, in Corden he's probably good as they get, I'd guess he'd do good almost anyplace. It kinda surprises me he's stayed here. Maybe he's just one of the kind that'd rather be the biggest frog in the small pond, you know?"

I wasn't sure, but then, I've never been able to understand the lawyering racket, let alone the guys that work it.

Back at the hotel Hazel was sitting in the parlor with Ma when I drifted in and gave her the story. She wasn't all that sure the father would have any more impact than the mother had on Ermine. Maybe less.

Ma asked me belligerently why Joey hadn't wanted Hazel along when we talked with Wes Nelson. I told her it was because he figured she'd distract the man, make him work too hard at impressing her to pay any attention to the problem we had with his daughter. That didn't impress Ma, but Hazel agreed it probably made sense.

"It isn't likely he'd ever have admitted he might not have complete control over his daughter if I'd been there." She smiled at me. "Your Joey's not as simple as he looks, is he?"

"I sure hope not."

Elihu had put Hazel in room ten, the best room in the house, and stuck me in room three, where I always bunked while working in the hotel. There was hardly room to stand between the single bed and the dresser. Even if Hazel hadn't been indisposed, we couldn't have managed anything; the floors squeaked so loud, the sound of my hike down that hall would have been enough to wake a drunk in the City Hall jail next door.

Not being able to bed together, we sat side by side in a couple of the lobby rockers after Ma and Elihu had retired to their room just beyond the hall. It was about as private as we could get.

"How you weathering the ancients?" I asked.

"Just fine. They're nowhere near as impossible as you'd have me believe. You shouldn't go out of your way to upset them."

"Never have to. I can manage that just breathing."

"I told your mother we were going to get married as soon as this thing with Derek gets sorted out."

"And she told you not to rush, right?"

Hazel laughed. "Yes, you could take it that way, I suppose. She pointed out that you're very much the traveling man, and hinted you might even be a trifle fickle. I'm trying to convince her you've just never met the right woman before."

"She ask you how come you married Derek?"

"Oh, yes, very casually. She wanted to know what attracted me to him most. I admitted it was a combination of personality and good looks. I was very young when we met, and easy to impress. He realized right away I was awed by professors, so he convinced me he was a big reader and a most promising scholar. What he was, was the total salesman, even back then. If he did approach Gwendolen, you can bet he convinced her he was whatever she wanted him to be. He had—I suppose still has—a genius for guessing what people want to hear, and making up his character to match. He could do it with either men or women, but he was best at it with women."

"So how come you've gone for me?"

"I'll probably never figure that out. Most likely it's because you're the absolute opposite of Derek. Absolutely no baloney. You're real as a rifle or a club—"

"And not too pretty?"

She laughed and touched my cheek.

"How'd he work on a girl like Dora Lynne?" I asked.

"Very simple. He'd just make her think she was beautiful, sexy, and generally irresistible. You know, she'd be the moon and stars, sunshine and hope, the girl of his dreams. He'd bury her under all that."

Sure. And when he'd visited me by the tent that night, he'd been the tough guy, with a cynic's view of women, but still unable to resist the appeal of a woman like Hazel. I was supposed to think we were two of a kind. Wouldn't a smart lawyer have a lovely time working with this son of a bitch? He could probably talk his way around any jury that ever assembled this side of hell.

≪ 29 ≫

t was 7:30 A.M. by my alarm clock when Pearl knocked on my door and said there was someone waiting in the lobby to talk with me.

"Who?" I mumbled.

"Says her name's Dora Lynne."

"I'll be down," I said, scrambling out from under the sheet over me.

It doesn't take long to get into my duds, but I had to stop at the toilet to be sure I had a clear mind for this meeting, and I even made a sashay into the shower room to comb my hair so I wouldn't be too severe a shock to the visitor. She was standing in the lobby near the window beside the front door, staring into the street, as I came in.

"Good morning," I said.

She turned quickly and moved away from the window.

"I'm sorry if I woke you—"

"Hey, no matter. Glad you came. Want some breakfast?"

"I'm not hungry—"

"So have a little coffee, or at least watch me take it—I need to clear the cobwebs this time of day."

She nodded solemnly and let me lead her through the vacant dining hall and out to the booth in the narrow room before the kitchen. After settling down, she gazed out the window on her right into the back lot of the hotel. It gave her a view of a clothes-line over a sandy area beside two big elms, and the back half of the brick wall of City Hall beyond. Her cheeks were carefully rouged and powdered, her pale eyebrows had been emphasized with a dark pencil, and she wore a pale shade of lipstick. None of those touches had been in evidence when I'd seen her before. I guessed even her eyelashes had been darkened. It seemed to make her blue eyes larger and brighter.

"You think you might've been followed?" I asked.

She looked startled, then closed her eyes and shook her head.

"Oh, no. He sleeps very hard in the morning."

"You mean Derek?"

She blushed. "Yes."

"Did he really marry you?"

Before she could answer, Pearl approached and asked what she'd like. Dora Lynne shook her head. I ordered orange juice, toast, and a cup of coffee for each of us, and when we were alone again repeated my question.

She hunched her shoulders and looked sorrowful.

"What's Derek done besides not keep his promise to marry you?"

Her eyes were leaking as she met my gaze. "Isn't that enough?"

"I kind of figure it's more than that, Dora Lynne. I'd guess you've found out he likes younger girls."

She dug a hankie from her purse and wiped her eyes carefully, then leaned against the booth back.

"When we were driving through here, a couple days back, he saw a young girl on the porch of a big house on Main Street, and right away he stopped. Just before that, he'd told me we weren't going to stop in Corden—he'd been there only a couple days before—but the moment he saw this young girl he pulled in and parked. And he went up to that house, leaving me just sitting in his car, and he talked to them for hours."

"You saw the mother come out?"

"No. But she came to the door after a while. Until then, Derek just sat on the porch railing there and talked with this young girl. I could just guess what he was telling her. When the older woman came in sight behind the screen, Derek and the girl went inside and I thought he'd spend the day in there."

"He sold them a set of encyclopedias."

"Well, yes, of course. But it needn't have taken that long. And the rest of the day he was impatient with me and hardly talked, and he's been like that ever since. It's like something is bothering him real bad, but he won't talk to me about it."

Pearl arrived with our breakfast, put it down, and left. I sugared and creamed my coffee and drank the orange juice. Dora Lynne sipped coffee and ignored the rest.

"Derek ever talk to you about young girls?" I asked.

"Of course not. But he never can keep from staring when he sees any."

"So why've you come to me?"

She put her cup down and leaned forward. "He told me you were after him. That you blame him for the murder of that girl in Jonesville."

"So now you want him caught?"

"He didn't kill that girl. Derek's not honest or faithful, but he'd never kill a girl. It's just not in him. He's not violent."

"So why're you turning him in?"

She drank some coffee, touched her mouth with her napkin, and slumped back.

"He knows who did it. You've got to talk to him, make him tell what he knows. Then he can get a divorce from that woman he's married to and marry me."

"How does Derek know who the killer was?"

"I'm not sure. He won't tell me any details, and I think it's because he's ashamed to have me know he was involved with that girl some way so he knew what happened. From things I've heard, I guess she was one of those kinds he gets excited about. The very pretty, terribly self-centered ones who love to believe all he tells them. Maybe, if he realizes the deep trouble all of that could get him into, he'll see he's been throwing himself away and should accept a woman like me, who really loves him and can make him happy."

"Dora Lynne, how'd you get here?"

"Well," she said, giving me a wide-eyed look, "I went to the gas station in town and talked with a man there, and he talked with a customer who was coming here and he gave me a ride."

"Who was he, and what town was this?"

"Just a man. I think Eliot, the fellow at the gas station in Raymond, called him Mr. Reeves or something. Anyway he was nice but didn't talk any, and he dropped me off out front."

"When was that?"

"Well, actually it was last night. Derek was drinking, and I got upset and decided to leave right away."

"So you spent the night in your apartment in Jonesville."

"That's right."

"You going to tell me where Derek is?"

"Will you go to see him alone?"

"I think I'd better tell Joey, our town cop, and the two of us will make the call."

"No, that'd panic him. I won't tell you where he is unless you promise to go alone. The house isn't in town, so you won't find it without me. Derek has heard you never use a gun, so he wouldn't be frightened if it was just you asking him the questions. You see, the man who really did it is a very prominent man in Jonesville and no one will want to go against him, but maybe you can, because you aren't scared of people with money and lots of friends—"

By this time I was wondering if Derek had been giving this woman lessons in salesmanship—or maybe she just learned by watching him operate. The only trouble was, I felt she didn't have his talent for kidding himself along with those he lied to, so she wasn't as convincing.

"Okay, where's the house?"

"Do you promise not to tell anyone else until you talk with him?"

"Sure."

"And you'll let me come along?"

"You want him to see you sicced me on him?"

"Well, it'll be for his own good, you can tell him that, can't you?"

"Okay. So where's the house?"

"It's an old farmhouse just a couple miles east of Raymond. Belonged to his aunt, who's not able to take care of herself and lives in Aquatown in an old folks' home. She said he could live there as long as he likes."

"Okay. Let's go."

⋘ 30 ⋙

We got to Raymond in jig time, and she directed me to a road running west. When I asked how come she'd told me earlier it was east, she said she got mixed up. It seemed likely that'd been a bum steer in case I broke my promise and tipped somebody off where we were going.

The first surprise was finding the house had been recently repainted. You just never saw a house with fresh paint in South Dakota these days, especially a farmhouse.

"How come?" I asked.

Dora Lynne almost smiled. "The paint job? Derek had it done before he'd move in. He's very neat."

Other than the finish, the farmhouse was much like every other one around: a two-story job with a steeply slanted roof, stingy overhang, and windows only at the gable end—none of your fancy dormers. There wasn't even a small roof over the front stoop. Dora Lynne approached the stoop directly, and I assumed Derek ignored the usual South Dakota farmer practice of using the front door for nothing but weddings and funerals.

"Where's his car?" I asked.

"He leaves it in the shed out back."

I suddenly realized there was no barn in sight and asked what had happened to that.

"It burned down this spring."

"Before or after the aunt went into the old folks' home?"

"I don't know—after, I think."

At the door she knocked, then turned the knob and stepped in. I followed. The living room extended the width of the house, slightly oblong, and was filled with furniture protected by anti-macassars and frilly woven covers. The lampshades had tassels; there was a big reddish carpet that covered the varnished floor to within a foot of the walls, and small red-and-black rugs along the area in front of the couch and the matching easy chair.

Dora Lynne called, "Derek?" and got no answer. She frowned and looked at me before going into the kitchen to the right. She emerged at once and went around to the door on the left, which I assumed was a bedroom.

"That's strange," she said as she came back out. She went to the stairway at the right end of the room, called "Derek!" again, and started up. I could hear her suddenly pause, then move about three steps. There was a cry, followed by a strange thump.

I went up, taking the steps three at a jump, spotted her on the floor beside a bed in the shaded room with a steeply sloping roof, and darted her way. Just before reaching her, I glanced at the bed and stopped short.

The head, with bulging eyes and protruding tongue, was deep in a white pillow. The covers were over the entire body but had been yanked free at the bottom, no doubt when his knees jerked up in his death struggle.

Dora Lynne moaned, and I knelt beside her and gently touched her forehead. Her eyes opened, wide with horror.

Eventually I got her to her feet and down the steps and asked if there was a telephone in the place. She shook her head. Her breath came in convulsive waves and she kept shaking her head in disbelief. I got her into the car and headed for town.

"Who else knew he was here?" I asked.

That got only another shake of her head. She suddenly sat up and looked in her lap.

"My purse," she said. "I—I must've dropped it."

"Want me to go back and get it?"

"Well, I've got to have it, haven't I?" She shuddered and put both hands to her face. "Oh God! He's dead! And I'm worried about my purse—"

I turned around, went back to the house, and got it for her. She waited in the car and seemed almost composed when I handed it over. She opened it, found a tiny handkerchief, and dabbed at her eyes as we headed back for town.

"I lied to you," she whispered. "He sent me to get you. He said you were a fool for women and it'd be easy to get your sympathy. He also said you were very clever at catching killers, and he'd convince you he hadn't done it to Gwendolen."

"So who did it? Sven?"

"I don't know. He never said. He claimed that Gwendolen invited him into the church, that it was her idea, and he went along because he didn't want to hurt her feelings. They were just talking, he said, when they heard someone come in upstairs, and she showed Derek a window he could climb out of there in the basement, and he ducked out through it and the next day heard about the murder. He claimed he never saw who it was—"

"You believe that?"

"I did. Now it doesn't seem likely, does it?"

We found the watchman in City Hall at Raymond. He was about ten years my senior, mostly bones, and gangly. His bright eyes took me in while I told him what was up. He blinked slowly now and then. Finally he suggested we ride out together and look things over. At first it seemed likely he'd invite me to wear cuffs for the trip, but Dora Lynne's backup of my story, and her upset state, made him sympathetic. He called home, talked to his wife, then drove Dora Lynne over there to wait for us. The wife was fat, squat, and happy-pumpkin-faced. She called her husband Slim and took Dora Lynne in like a long-lost daughter. I went back out with Slim to his Model A and sat by his side, freehanded, for the ride back to the scene of the crime. Inside the house he carefully took down notes on the body, the room, and eventually the whole place, moving about slowly and checking drawers. He checked out the basement last. It was a dugout affair, with nothing but a coal furnace and a small coal bin to one side. While we poked around, he questioned me about Derek's background and the Gwendolen murder.

Then we went outside and checked on the car in the shed. It was a recent-model Olds, four-door, in gray.

"What do you figure happened in there?" he asked me as we drove back to arrange for a pickup of the body and an examination by a doctor.

"Somebody caught him asleep, straddled him, pinning his arms under the blankets, and strangled him to death."

He nodded.

"Any notion who?"

"Well, I'm damn sure it wasn't the girlfriend—she's too lightweight to hold him down, and besides, why'd she lead me out to him?"

He nodded. "Figure it could've been that Sven guy, the brother?"

"Maybe. He's sure healthy enough and maybe mean enough —but I can't quite figure the why. It isn't like he was crazy about his sister. Far as I know, he never met Derek or heard anything about him. Of course, I can't know that's a fact."

"I guess you been in on a few murders before."

"That's not quite it—I've investigated some. You ever had any?"

"Once. Five years ago. When Nan Tucker whacked her hubby with an ax after he got drunk and beat hell out of her. She come to, found him drunk asleep, went out to the woodshed, got the ax, came back, and let him have it. No mystery there. She came straight to me and laid it out."

"And went to prison?"

"She says it's better than living with him."

Not poetic, but justice of a kind.

≪ 31 ≫

The next morning at breakfast I told Hazel we had to stop by and see my old friend Boswell before we left town.

She wanted to know, naturally, who he was, and I explained how he had been, among other things, the town's only bootlegger through Prohibition, but before that was a railroad man and for a time after his retirement janitored at the high school.

"Doesn't he have a first name?"

"If he does, nobody I know's ever heard it."

It was about ten-thirty when we strolled south from the hotel, crossed the railroad track, and walked parallel with them to the old man's shack, which stood about a dozen yards south of the line. I explained to Hazel that he'd built it with salvaged boxcar remnants from a wreck long ago.

We found him sitting in a wooden chair beside his front door, smoking his reeking, stubby pipe and sipping coffee from a large brown mug. As always, he had a stubble beard, bloodshot eyes, untrimmed white hair, and a broad smile. I could never figure how he always looked as if he hadn't shaved for a week; I guessed he must trim it every day or so with dull scissors.

He climbed to his unsteady feet, greeted Hazel warmly with his old eyes, and grasped my hand as I made introductions.

"What's your first name?" Hazel asked.

"Ignatius," he said.

"You never told me that," I complained.

He shrugged, grinned, and asked us inside. I knew it wasn't to show off his cluttered place; his problem was he had only two chairs, and for three people he had to use the bed for the third sitter. Hazel made a point of not staring around at the room's total chaos, accepted a cup of coffee without flinching, and took the chair he'd brought in from outside and offered her. He sat on a stool and waved me to the bed.

We gassed a bit about some common friends before I finally got down to cases and asked how much he knew about the lawyer Wes Nelson.

"Well, he never bought any moon off me. Guess he makes out pretty good. Got a perky daughter and a smart wife."

"Ever hear of Derek Warford?"

"Oh yah, the traveling man from Sioux Falls."

"How'd you happen to hear about him?"

"He come regular for moonshine back when I was sellin'. Figured he must peddle it, since he took more than any man could drink by himself."

"Give him a good price?"

"Gave everybody a good price. Nobody different."

"Ever hear he owned a farm over near Raymond?"

"He didn't own it—belonged to his old aunt Leck. Made deliveries there a few times way back. She never wanted anybody to know, and I never told. Crusty old woman. Hear she went to an old folks' home a while back and suppose the nephew keeps it up now. Haven't been around there in a coon's age."

As we walked back to the hotel, Hazel asked me if I thought Boswell had liked her.

"Sure."

"How could you tell?"

"I don't know. He just looked happy about you."

"Did he meet your wife when she came to Corden?"

"Yeah. Once."

"How'd he look at her?"

"Well, he just looked sad."

She laughed and squeezed my arm.

"You almost always say just the right thing," she said.

"Almost?"

"Who could ask for more?"

« 32 »

azel and I checked out of the Wilcox Hotel after lunch with Ma and Elihu. Both of them made it clear they'd be happy to see her again. I didn't detect any strong sentiment for my return, but they seemed more tolerant than usual. Elihu even hinted that the boy working for them would be going back to school in September and wondered idly if I'd be coming around in the fall. I said it would depend, and he didn't ask on what. The one thing I could be sure of around them was no excess sentimentality.

Before taking us back to Jonesville, I swung around to Raymond for talks with Dora Lynne and Slim. Slim said we were both free to go, but we should let him know where we could be reached if anything developed on the murder. The only sure thing at that point was that Derek had been strangled by someone who left no tracks. As far as Dora Lynne could determine, nothing had been stolen from the house, and they found Derek's wallet on the bureau beside the bed with cash and identification complete, plus forty-five cents in loose change.

When I offered Dora Lynne a ride to Jonesville, she said no, that was the last place she wanted to see right now. She'd get a bus to Aquatown and talk with a man she knew who might be able to give her a job in a beauty parlor there.

Hazel and I got back to Jonesville before suppertime and looked up Officer Driscoll to fill him in on everything except my morning's visit with Boswell. He said he'd never met Slim but hadn't heard any bad reports on him, which only suggested he hadn't made any mouthy enemies.

"So," said Driscoll, "we're down to Sven or Doc Westcott."

"May be."

"Who else has a motive? They're bound to figure he had to be the killer—it'd be enough to make any relative go nuts."

"If it was like that, I'd guess Sven would be most likely, being young and hotheaded. A few days ago he took a crack at me, so I know how he moves when he's mad. And from all we've been told, Doc Westcott wouldn't be as likely to know what was going on with Gwendolen. But there's a little hitch. How'd either one of them know where to find Derek, even if they knew who he was, which we can't be sure of right now?"

"Well, around here there aren't many secrets. We've just got to talk to the right people for leads."

"You know if Sven's got a special girlfriend?" I asked.

"Seems like I heard he used to be kind of involved with Ida Todd, whose daddy runs the drugstore where she clerks now and again. They were classmates in high school, but I think they went to different colleges this year."

Todd's Drugstore was in the middle of the block on Main Street. Things were quiet when I walked in and strolled between high-shelved aisles to the back, where a chubby senior was bending down, looking at a shelf behind the counter. His bald spot was a perfect circle in the center of his skull and had a fine gray-haired frame. When he looked up, I could take in his full gray mustache and watery blue eyes under bushy brows.

"Mr. Todd?" I asked.

"In the ample flesh," he told me solemnly. "What can I do for you?"

I glanced past him and to the right, where a young woman was writing something on what I assumed was a prescription label.

I told him my name and gave him a vague explanation of my job. He nodded, obviously not surprised, and asked how he could help me.

"Introduce me to your daughter."

"I think she's a bit young for you."

"I can see that from here, but what I want to do is ask her a couple questions about a friend of hers, if you don't mind."

He turned and called, "Ida."

She looked up, took me in, glanced at him, and walked toward us. Her blue-gray eyes were average size, but the lashes were extra long and black. Her eyebrows had been plucked into thin lines, and her mouth was generously lipsticked and ripe. She offered a polite smile. Her father told her I was the detective guy from Corden that Sven had been seeing more of than he wanted to.

The eyes became a little larger. She said, "How do you do," obviously without expecting an account.

I explained some of the problems in the case we were working on and told her that since the whole business was so mixed up, I had to ask a lot of questions that normally wouldn't be anybody's business, trying to pick up hints that would give explanations for what had happened to Gwendolen Westcott. She took that in, and said, "For instance?"

"Was Sven with you the night she died?"

"Does he need an alibi?"

"We have to know everything possible about anybody related, by blood or anything else, so we can narrow the thing down and maybe reach answers. You want to answer my question?"

"He wasn't with me."

"He ever talk to you about his sister?"

"Not much. I'm not sure why, but I always had a notion he had guilt feelings about her. When they were real young, I mean, somewhere like four and six, up to when he was eleven, they were real close. Then his father let him know he was being too mother-hennish, and he got all upset and just practically broke off with her. He told me she was real hurt for a long time, and then when she got older, she seemed to hold it against him. By the time she was in high school she just snubbed him something awful. He couldn't deal with it."

"Did it make him mad?"

"Oh no, that wasn't it. Actually he seemed to just feel guilty and sort of, you know, sad. Actually it kind of made me like him better. I mean, he doesn't seem sensitive if you don't know him, because he always puts on this real tough front, but really he's sort of a cream puff."

"How'd he feel about her hanging on teachers and the Bible school guy?"

"He tried to pretend he never noticed, but I think he resented them real bad. When I first knew him our junior year, he tried to tell her she shouldn't get all involved with those people, but she told him flat out it was none of his business, and he just gave up on her."

"You see much of him lately?"

"Not since our senior year. We were together a lot then, but after graduation, when we went to different towns for college, it never amounted to much. We haven't dated this summer."

"Who does he see?"

"I don't know," she said, and glanced at her father. "Have you heard?"

"You think I've time for gossip?" he asked, raising his bushy brows.

"I think you set regular schedules for it."

He grinned and looked at me. "Why do you want to know who he's involved with?"

"To learn as much about the guy as I can. I've talked with him two or three times and get mixed signals. He seems like a lonely guy."

"He is," said Ida. "You've got that right."

"Well, he's not always lonely. From what I hear, he's a mite involved with a fine cook," said Todd.

"Really?" asked Ida. "Who in the world?"

"Better you should ask, who in Jonesville?"

"All right, who?"

"How many famous cooks've we got?"

Ida frowned, then her eyebrows rose.

"Oh, come on, she's old enough to be his mother."

"Not quite."

"Who?" I asked.

"Don't pay him any attention—he's just pulling your leg. Why, Sven would die at the very suggestion—"

"That's why it's such a secret," said Todd, still grinning.

"Are you talking about Purita, the hotel cook?" I asked.

"Who else?" His grin was practically wall-to-wall.

"Look, this isn't a kidding deal, you know? Be serious."

"Okay," he said. "I'm kidding. How'd I know anything about the love life of our doctor's son?"

"Dad," said Ida, "cut it out. You probably know more gossip than any man in town—"

"Man or woman," he agreed.

"How'd a guy like Sven ever get at somebody like Purita?" Ida asked. "I've heard she never leaves the hotel."

"Purita has become more active since you went to college, dearie. She's been persuaded by Pastor Bjornson to handle church suppers during the last year. And so she spends a bit of time in the church basement kitchen and dining area, and guess who cleans it up? And guess who are the last two people to leave that basement on church supper nights? I've even heard they take evening walks together."

"Come on! A fellow like Sven would never get involved with a woman like Purita—"

"Who knows what she's like? So she's a big woman, a little awkward, not a raving beauty. But she *is* a woman, and she's lived alone a long time since she came to marry a man who failed to claim her. And Sven's had no girl he's been involved with since you."

"I can't believe it."

"But you can believe if he did get involved with Purita, he wouldn't exactly advertise it, right?"

She didn't argue. I thanked them both and left.

❄ 33 ❄

hat evening Hazel and I ate in the hotel restaurant.

"Well," I said, "now it's safe for you to move back with Abigail Smith."

She gave me a lowered-eyebrow look and asked if that was what I really wanted.

"No. I don't think she'd let me in her place. And I don't think I'd care to if she did. You want to get married tomorrow?"

"Who've you got in mind for me?"

"Somebody thick-skinned enough to marry a lady who's only been a widow two days."

"There aren't many like that around."

"I'll bet you could find a dozen in Jonesville. Not because there're that many tough guys around, but because you're such a dish. I'm on the level. You willing to do it?"

"You're just saying that because you know I'm through with my period and ready again. How'll you feel in a month?"

"That'll be up to you. I should be tired enough by then to coast a few days."

"Actually," she said, drawing up a little, "I don't feel much like kidding about this business right now."

"I'm not kidding. You say yes, and we do it, go back to Corden, and take over the hotel. You like Min and Elihu, right? They like you. The place is getting to be too much for the old man, and Ma'd be happy playing bridge and socializing more with her church crowd. It won't last long—I mean the hotel—but I can get it fixed up enough with apartments to unload to somebody and get a stake and then we move on."

"To what?"

"I don't know. I'll have to work on it."

"I don't want a justice-of-the-peace marriage. It should be in a place that means something to us, with guests, not just witnesses."

"Okay."

She reached across the table, and I met her hand with mine.

"Really?" she asked.

"Sure. Where've you got in mind?"

"How about the Wilcox Hotel?"

I laughed. "You really know how to make a hit with the old folks, don't you? Sure, why not?"

"We'll do it in September."

After dinner we walked around town and sat at a picnic table in the park, taking advantage of the warm, still evening and the fact that we didn't have to wonder if Derek might be lurking somewhere near. If we'd been in Corden, I'd have suggested we go out to the swimming hole and take a dip, but Jonesville had no comparable pool available. A little after ten we returned to the hotel and went to bed in her room. I suppose it was the calmest night of lovemaking we had known up till then, but it was the coziest too.

When we were having breakfast in the morning, Jud Pickett came to our table to tell me the Reverend Bjornson had called and asked me to come around to the parsonage as soon as it was convenient.

"I guess," the pastor said when I was seated in the straight-backed chair before his desk, "I owe you one hundred dollars."

"There's no absolute proof that Derek did it," I said.

"Well, I'm satisfied he did, so I'm obliged to make it right with you as agreed."

"Even if I keep on doing some investigating?"

"To what end?"

"Well, Reverend, Derek couldn't quite manage to strangle himself. It was done to him. It seems like somebody ought to find out who managed it. Especially since we don't have any real evidence Derek killed Gwendolen. It seems most likely he'd been overfamiliar with her, but there's no reason for us to believe he killed her. He messed with a lot of girls and never, so far as I can find, even so much as slapped one of them."

"No doubt that's because none of the other girls spurned him, which I'm confident was the case with Gwendolen. She was a flirt, not a wanton."

"Have it your way, Reverend. You going to pay in cash or with a check?"

"I can give you a check now, or pay cash this afternoon—whichever you prefer."

He laboriously wrote out a check for $75, taking off the $25 he had advanced after my car was wrecked, carefully tore it free, and handed it over. I thanked him, took it, and went to the bank and asked for seven tens and five ones. All but the ones looked like they'd been printed that morning.

I was on my way back to the hotel to show Hazel her dowry when I met Officer Driscoll on the street. He invited me back to his office in City Hall, where we plunked down in chairs and he scowled at me.

"All settled with the reverend?" he asked.

"He seems to think so."

"But we still got a little problem here, haven't we?"

"How do you see it, beyond the fact we don't know if Derek killed Gwendolen and haven't nailed whoever did in Derek?"

"Have you asked yourself who could've known where Derek was hiding out?" he asked.

"Dora Lynne knew. And anybody else she told."

"But nobody else?"

"Come on, Driscoll, you've got a notion, spit it out."

"Your lady friend, Hazel. It just could be she knew that her husband had an old aunt who left her farmhouse to him just a ways from Corden."

"How'd Hazel know about that farm?"

"Well, just because he didn't tell his wife about the girls he laid doesn't mean the rest of his life was a secret to her."

"She left him two years ago. He wasn't using that place then."

"We don't know that for a fact. Maybe he was taking young girls out there regular. But even if he wasn't, Hazel could still know it was there and figure out it'd be a good hideout, even if the aunt was still around."

"Can you picture a gal Hazel's size sitting on Derek's chest and strangling him while he kindly let her?"

"If she found him passed out, sat with her knees pinning his arms down, yeah, she probably could've managed it."

"Why the hell would she do it now?"

"Well, maybe the opportunity never came by before. Maybe she was going nuts wanting to marry her cowboy boyfriend. Or maybe she hired somebody."

"Sure, she's just loaded with dough from her teaching job in this burg. You're blowing wind. What you don't want to do is look at your town's only doctor, or his son, who're the only real candidates for a murder rap."

"Uh-uh. Neither of them would know where he was, even if they were in the mood for murder. And a guy like Doc sure's hell would never do it. He's never done anything to anybody but try to keep them alive, healthy, and paying doctor bills."

"The doc probably knows more about people in and around this town than you or I or anybody else."

"No, there you're wrong. Doc Westcott's not one of your palsy medicine men. He's all business. No gossip. That's what most people around here like about him—he is all the way the professional man. He prides himself on it."

I allowed as how he probably knew the man better than I did. Driscoll glowed a little but didn't push it.

A telephone call to Raymond got me Slim, who reported that the local doc had examined Derek and said yeah, the victim had been drinking, probably most of the night, so he'd not likely been what you'd call real alert when the killer parked on his chest. No, he couldn't tell how big the hands were that strangled him.

Back in the hotel Purita was starting to prepare lunch when I ambled in and leaned against the counter where she was making a tuna salad.

"You happen to know Doc Westcott?" I asked.

"Everybody in Jonesville knows him," she said, not looking up.

"Been his patient?"

"A time or two."

"Anything serious?"

She looked up from the mixing bowl and finally said he had operated on her for a hernia two years back.

"I didn't know women got them," I admitted.

"Oh, we're not that much different."

"What do you think of the doctor?"

She shrugged, very casually, and said he seemed to know what he was doing.

"You know his son?"

Her eyes narrowed before she smiled thinly.

"Yes. He works at the church. I've cooked there. We see each other often."

"He ever talk about his sister?"

It was plain this wasn't a direction she expected me to take, but she only hesitated a moment before answering.

"Not much."

"What does he talk about?"

"Well, sometimes he asks if there's anything I want him to do, like carry the garbage out or do I need more potatoes. We don't have a whole lot of time for chatter."

"What was the name of the guy you came here to marry?"

Again she hesitated before answering. "The name on the mailings I got was David Worton."

"And he didn't show up to meet you at the train?"

"He may have been there. Quite a few men were standing around, but none of them stepped forward."

"You ever see a picture of him?"

She shook her head. "All I had was a letter that claimed he owned a house and I would have a rich life."

"Where'd he say this house was?"

"He didn't say. I just figured it was here in Jonesville."

"You ever see Derek Warford when he stayed at the hotel?"

"You asked me that before, and I said no. He didn't come out to the kitchen, and I don't roam out into the dining room or peek through the door. I'm too busy for that nonsense."

"And I don't imagine guests show up at church suppers?"

"I'd not likely know if they did. Wouldn't know a guest from a member."

"You do any cooking at the church last night?"

"No, I didn't. Now, I've no more time for talk, I've got to fix lunch."

I gave up and went back to the lobby.

≪ 34 ≫

Jud Pickett was talking with a salesman when I entered the lobby, but that ended when the guy went up to his room. I asked if Pearl lived in the hotel. He said no, she boarded with her parents on the north side of town.

"You know if Purita went anyplace last night?"

"No. She doesn't have to check in and out."

"What does she do evenings?"

"Now and again she goes over to the church and cooks dinners. Outside of that, I wouldn't know. I don't go up to check her room."

"When she goes out, does she leave through here?"

"She does when she goes to the church, yeah. But she could just as easy use the back door. It's never locked."

"She ever say anything to you about the guy that jilted her when she came to town?"

"Nope. It wasn't a thing she ever wanted to chat up."

"How'd you know what happened?"

"Well, she asked around at the depot about this fella that was supposed to meet her. Told the depot manager, Brady, she was expected. Happens I know Brady, and when he got talking with her while she waited there, he found out she'd been a cook out east, and knowing I was in need, he brought her over."

"She talk good English then?"

"Oh yeah. Not quite so good as now, but nobody ever had any trouble understanding Purita. She's real quick, that one. We didn't talk more'n fifteen minutes when I offered her the job. She said she'd take it. Been here ever since."

"Is Brady still around?"

"Nope. Died of a heart attack last year."

Another dead end.

Hazel and I went to eat lunch at the café down the street.

I told her about my talk with Purita and the follow-up with Jud Pickett, and then we discussed the notion of romance between Sven and Purita.

"I can't picture it," she said. "She doesn't strike me as the sort of woman who'd get involved with somebody who was practically a juvenile, and I can't believe he has enough imagination to appreciate a woman who's older than he is and almost as tall."

"How about the doc? You believe he could go for her?"

"Ah. There's a thought. He operated on her, didn't he? That hardly seems like a great beginning for romance, but on the other hand, somehow I can imagine it. For an older man there would be something a little exotic about this foreign woman who is obviously unfulfilled. And his own wife is completely conventional, don't you think?"

"Yeah. And I've got the notion they're pretty far apart on how to handle the kids. It could have been a real sore spot between them. If she made him feel guilty about how he handled them, that could cut things off good."

She leaned forward, all bright-eyed. "That's right. You have a man like the doctor, who thinks of himself as pretty godlike, and his wife starts to treat him like he's less than perfect, you can bet he'll be vulnerable for romance, and the partner he'll likely choose will be as different as possible to the one he's obligated to."

"I suppose."

She grinned at me. "You think I read too many books, don't you?"

"I guess you wouldn't have to read books to get ideas, you do fine studying people."

She patted her mouth with a napkin and sat back, smiling cozily. "Who're you going to grill next?"

"You."

"Shoot."

"Driscoll's got some ideas of his own about all this. He wonders if you knew about Derek's aunt and the farmhouse."

The smile faded. "Why's he wonder about that?"

"Well, there's this question about how the killer managed to find Derek. It seems like not everybody knew about his little hideout, or how long he'd been using it over the years. He ever take you there before you were married, or after?"

"No. But I vaguely remember him mentioning a widowed aunt who had a farm and was living there alone for a time. He even mentioned he'd be the heir. He kidded about it, calling it the family plantation. But I never knew the location, and don't think he visited it."

"And you never did?"

"Never."

"So you couldn't tell anybody else where it was. Even accidentally."

"No. I had no interest and no reason, and I'm sure you know that."

"That's what I told Driscoll. But it didn't seem too smart not to get straight with you on it. I figure if there was any time when you felt like killing him, it would have been when you found him with his girlie on the couch. If you didn't whack him to death then, I sure can't picture you climbing on his bunk and doing the job bare-handed at this late date."

"But maybe I arranged for somebody else to do it, is that in the back of your dirty little mind?"

"Pretty far back."

She grinned again. "I know what's going on in your head. You're beginning to panic at the notion of getting married, so you're groping for escape routes."

"Well, whenever I think about how great you are at loving, and how much fun I have just talking with you, I get this nagging notion that maybe you're too good to be true. Can you cook?"

"Now we're really getting down to basics, huh? Yes, I can, and most of the time I really enjoy it. You cook some yourself, don't you?"

"Yup. First roundup I was on, they hired me to take over the chuck wagon. Learned to cook from Ma. Too bad it wasn't from Bertha, but she came later. Let's take a walk."

"Where are we going?"

"Thought we might stop by where Kilbride's staying and talk a minute."

"You've got ideas about him?"

"Just a question to ask."

His landlady told us he was over at the park, and we strolled that way. The wind blew Hazel's hair across her face, and she pushed it back and squinted against the glaring sunlight. We found Kilbride sitting alone on a bench by a softball diamond where a small group of teenagers were playing ball. He sighted us at once, smiled, and stood up as we approached.

"I don't suppose you realize," he said, "that actually I'm a scout for the Minneapolis Millers, out here checking on prospects."

"See anybody promising?" I asked.

"Several. But I'm not saying anything yet—don't want to build false hopes. You ever play any ball?"

"Just work-up," I said.

"What's that?" asked Hazel.

"When there are too few kids to make up teams, they draw straws to see who bats, then another for pitcher, catcher, and so on. If the batter strikes out, flies out, or gets tagged, he goes to the field and works up to his turn at bat again."

We sat down on the bench with Hazel in the middle and I asked how he got the note he received after Gwendolen's death.

Kilbride frowned. "It came by regular mail in a cream-colored envelope, carefully printed address, no return. The stationery inside matched the envelope. The printing was the same inside and out. Very precise."

"Postmark?"

"Jonesville."

"Was Zelda in your Bible class?"

"Yes. But only the first week. She dropped out."

"Anybody tell you why?"

"I was told she has a problem periodically with headaches. That was her mother's story. I never had a chance to talk with Zelda about it, and it bothered me because her mother gave me the feeling the headache was my fault. Rather upsetting, you know?"

No, he had never noticed any relations between Zelda and Gwendolen. They sat well apart and paid no attention to each other.

We left him and went around to Dr. Westcott's house. His wife, Martha, answered my knock and gave Hazel a look considerably shy of approval. I asked if she'd be kind enough to answer a couple questions.

"What about?"

"You ever notice any mail to Sven or your husband this past summer without a return address?"

"What a strange question. Why do you ask?"

"Chris Kilbride got a weird note right after Gwendolen's death. It seemed like whoever wrote that one might have written some others. It could give us a line on what happened later."

"Well, I go over all the mail that comes, and I don't remember anything like that."

"The note to Kilbride came on a cream-colored envelope with a neatly hand-printed address. You don't remember any?"

"I've already told you, no."

"Sorry. It's just important to get things clear as possible in a murder case, and that makes the questions pretty tiresome. Can you tell me where your husband and Sven were the night of the murder?"

"I've told Officer Driscoll already."

"Okay, so do me a favor and do it again, please?"

She lifted her chin and said, "Sven was home all evening and went to his room a little after ten. We'd been listening to the radio—"

"What'd you hear?"

"Well, there was *Lum and Abner*, and *Cecil and Sally*—"

"They're on pretty early, aren't they?"

"Well, later we listened to some music. What difference does it make?"

"It narrows time down. Where was the doctor?"

"He was out on a call."

"When did he leave?"

"It was just a bit after supper."

"Who answered the phone?"

"Sven. He told his father it was a woman."

"No name?"

There was almost a pause before she answered that she didn't recall. If he gave one, it didn't mean anything to her.

"Could it have been Purita?"

Martha scowled at me. "Why would it be her?"

"Why not? She'd been a patient before, hadn't she?"

"Well, I suppose it could have been, but it's unlikely. The doctor has treated hundreds of patients."

"Of course. Did he tell you what the emergency was?"

"No. He said it was north of town—"

"Did he take notes when people called?"

"Only when he wasn't familiar with where they lived. Most of the time he knows about mothers because they've been to see him during pregnancy. But now and then some farmer's wife just hasn't ever bothered. Some of them don't want to pay money until they have to."

"And sometimes they can't pay when they do call, right?"

Her eyes lost a shade of their hostility, and she almost smiled. "Yes, you're right. He often settles for milk, vegetables, eggs, and chickens instead of cash."

"What did he bring back this time?"

"Well"—the hostility was back—"I've no idea—he sends a bill—"

"He handle his own books?"

"Of course."

I thanked her, and we left.

"What do you think?" I asked Hazel.

"I think she's heard we're having an affair."

"Yeah, but about the mail—"

"I wouldn't make any bets, one way or the other."

"All of a sudden she's hostile. She wasn't like that before."

"Well, now she's probably afraid you're suspicious of her men. That sort of thing can change a mother's attitude in a hurry."

"You know something? I don't think she'd worry a whole lot if we were suspicious of her hubby."

"That's why you asked her about Purita, isn't it? To see if she knew something may have been going on between them."

"Yeah, let's go talk with her."

"I think maybe it's not a good idea for me to be in on these things. Women particularly resent me. I'll go back to the school library, and you pick me up there later, okay?"

I accepted that and walked back to the hotel, thinking how much easier things had been when I handled cases where there were bona fide bastards involved, like Bo, the guy who killed little Alma. Messing with prominent citizens was nothing but a mess of tiptoeing around.

⤙ 35 ⤚

urita was sitting at the table by the window in her kitchen when I walked in. She frowned as I settled into the chair across from her.

"I've been talking to Mrs. Westcott," I said.

All that got me was raised eyebrows.

"I got a little notion while talking with her that she figures her hubby's got a special interest in another woman."

She pulled back a little. "I suppose you encouraged that?"

"Nope. Never raised the notion or offered a hint. But it's there. It'd be real natural that Gwendolen's killing would jolt the doc out of his regular ruts, sort of get him taking a new look at his life. When we talked a while back, he told me he'd come to realize he knew more about his family's innards than he did about their minds. I think he looked into his wife's head and didn't find much he wanted. I think maybe he's been going out nights more to do what makes babies than to deliver them, you know?"

"Well, I guess you know something about that sort of business. What's it got to do with me?"

"That's just one of the things I'm trying to figure out. Like whether it was him that told you that the man who sent for you as a bride was Derek Warford, or did you just happen to overhear Dora Lynne and her friend gossiping about it?"

"How would any of them know that?"

"I figure Derek was the kind of ass who'd think that whole thing was funny and couldn't resist blabbing about it. It'd give the doc a double motive for wanting to settle his hash, and it'd sure as hell make you boil, so maybe it was you that did the bastard in. Or tipped off the doc on where he might find him so he could do it."

"You have a great imaginatio.n I suppose you think if you can make me a suspect, I'll tell on the doctor to save myself. Is that the trick?"

"I might try that. Or tell him we've got a case against Sven. I think that'd work even better."

"Yes, it probably would. Even fathers who can't understand their sons can't help trying to protect them. Why don't you just go back to Corden and leave us all alone?"

"It's tempting. But Driscoll's not going away. This is murder in his territory, and he's the cop in charge. He has to do something."

"Like find a goat."

"You've got it. I'd rather he picked the real killer, whoever it is, than settle on a patsy."

"Like me."

"Well, you'd make a lot more popular choice for him than the only doctor in town. Or his only son. How'd the doc find out where Derek was?"

She sighed, shook her head, and finally slumped in her chair.

"He got a letter."

"Anonymous, right?"

"Yes."

"Cream envelope, printed message?"

"If you know everything, why do you keep asking questions?"

"Just want to firm it up. Did you get one of the notes too?"

"You're fantastic. Are you going to see Dr. Westcott?"

"Not yet. First I'll try another angle. And Purita, don't make any sudden trips, okay?"

Her expression didn't tell me whether she thought that was a hint in the opposite direction or not. There was almost a smile on her wide mouth when I glanced back before going out.

Zelda answered my knock on the Johnsons' door. I asked if we could talk. She said not in the house, since her mother was downtown, but she'd sit with me on the porch. If my visit surprised or worried her, she hid it well. She smoothed her skirt over her slender legs and crossed her ankles after taking a chair to my right. Her hair was not as tightly marcelled as before, and I liked it better almost loose. The street before us was deserted, there wasn't a car moving or parked in sight, and the sidewalks in both directions were shady and vacant.

"I've been a little disappointed that I haven't had any anonymous letters," I said.

She lifted one eyebrow. "Why do you say that?"

"Well, the missionary got one a while back, the doc got his just lately, and I think a third one went to Purita. It seems about my turn."

"I don't know what you're talking about."

"I guess none of them got a lot of general notice. How'd you learn about Derek Warford's farmhouse?"

"You're talking in riddles."

"Come on, Zelda, you're the greatest little figure-outer in Jonesville, maybe the whole state. How often do you get your hair fixed?"

Her mouth sagged a second as her eyes widened.

"What do you care?"

"You used to go to Dora Lynne's shop, didn't you?"

She hesitated, decided that'd be too easy for me to check if she denied it, and said yes, so what?

"So I think you got her talking, and she told you things about Derek Warford. Like the fact he was interested in her and what a great salesman he was and how he had this farm not far away from Jonesville. Right?"

"What if she did?"

"Well, if she admitted to it, and I'll be checking with her on it, then it would seem pretty likely that you wrote one of your neat little letters to the good doctor, telling him where he could find the man who murdered his daughter."

"You won't be able to prove that, and if you talk to anybody about it, my father will make lots of trouble for you."

"Oh, it won't be a matter of gossip. And far as I know, there's no law against writing little notes to people and forgetting to sign your name. What I'm after is nailing down a case against the guy who really strangled Derek, so some innocent goat doesn't get sacrificed."

Her eyes never wavered, but something close to a smile showed up for a moment.

"Who do you think might be the goat?"

"There are at least two possibles—Sven and Purita, the cook at the hotel. Of course, Sven doesn't make a very good goat, since he's the doctor's son as well as the pastor's nephew. A lot more popular goat would be Purita, who has no high-powered relatives, and I suppose about everybody knows that Derek was the guy who brought her out here with a marriage offer and jilted her when she showed up. Driscoll might make a case that she stored up her mad-on and settled his hash when he was sleeping off a drunk. He might have a little trouble making a case for how she got out there, but that could probably be worked out. She's a real healthy woman and could probably have hiked the distance if there was no other choice."

"You like her?"

"I like her better than Sven or the doc."

"You like her better than Hazel?"

"I don't like anybody better than Hazel. Why?"

"She could be a goat too. I bet she hated Derek. And she's another outsider."

"Yeah. But she's kind of small for the job, and she's been with me too steady to go off strangling anybody without any wheels of her own. How about we quit kidding around and you just level with me?"

"Because I've nothing to tell, and even if I did, I'm not going to get into any trouble about all this. You can't prove anything."

"Oh, did you wear gloves when you wrote the notes?"

"You don't have any of them."

"You can't be sure of that."

She laughed. "I am now. If you had one, you'd have said so."

"Okay, just between you and me, which of them did you write to, the doc or Sven?"

"If I knew anything and was going to write to anybody, it would be the doctor."

"Well, all right, then."

She stood up when I did and stopped by the door.

"Are you going to tell my mother anything?"

"Not now. It's just possible, knowing what I do, a little talk with the doctor will settle things. We'll see. And don't worry about the doctor too much. I won't tell him who his anonymous writer was unless I really have to."

That scared her, but she didn't try to stop me when I left, and it didn't make me feel a damned bit sorry if she was going to sweat. It seemed like she deserved at least some of that.

≪ 36 ≫

I made sure the doc was in his office late in the afternoon and hung around the street until he came out at about six. He moved like a sleepwalker and didn't notice me until he stopped at the street corner and I stepped up beside him.

"Don't suppose you ever have a drink in public, do you, Doc?"

He started, almost as though I'd poked him in the kidneys, froze for a second, then said no in a whisper.

"You mind swinging by the park before you go home? I got a serious problem and need your help."

He took a deep breath before asking, "Why is your problem mine?"

"Well, you're the biggest part of it. First, I can't figure why you went through your daughter's room and got rid of all her letters and diaries the day after she died. It had to be you or Sven, but somehow Sven doesn't seem right for it, and you were the guy that made up her room after she was gone. That really impressed your lady. Says you never did anything like that before in your life. How come you did that?"

He shook his head and started walking.

"You see," I said, keeping in step, "it comes down to one of three people that strangled Derek Warford. Now, it's just natural that the cop in a town like this isn't likely to put the finger on the town's only medic, especially since he's a man about every other citizen in town figures is the most important guy within fifty miles of any direction. So the patsy in this case is going to wind up either being your son or your girlfriend, Purita. I don't think you're the kind of guy who'd let somebody else take the rap for you, especially not your own kid, or almost as bad, your girlfriend. Am I wrong?"

He kept walking, his head thrust forward, his shoulders high. We crossed the street and entered a small park, with a quarter of a block on the southeast section covered by small, neatly planted elms in long rows. The rest was all softball fields. Under the trees there were picnic tables and a few small fireplaces for charcoal or kindling fires. The doctor sat down on a picnic table bench and stared across the playing fields.

"I don't believe," he said, "that a case can be made against Sven or Purita."

"A smart prosecutor wouldn't have much trouble making a case for the theory that this foreign woman who'd been tricked into taking a train to the boondocks, then got jilted, would want to smash this bug who'd been bragging about making a fool of her while he ran around screwing fourteen-year-old girls. And it'd be even easier to make his case if he could prove that Purita had been in love with the father whose daughter this guy had strangled in a church basement. Especially if she kept getting goosed by anonymous letters written by a schoolmate of Gwendolen's, who hated her and her family."

He shook his head.

"This can't happen," he said. His voice was barely audible.

"It's going to."

"Does Driscoll know of the anonymous notes?" he asked.

"Only about the one to the Bible school man. So far."

"You know who wrote them?"

"Yup."

He sat edgeways on the bench and doubled over as if he had a stomachache, except he kept his head up and stared into the vacant playing field.

"The most awful thing," he said, "is that he didn't even kill Gwendolen. It was his fault, but he didn't do it. I did."

"What happened, Doc? Did you catch her with Derek and go nuts?"

"I got a call. It told me I should go see what my daughter was doing in the basement of the church. I told Martha it was a call from a woman having a baby, and I left. The church was dark, and when I turned on the stairway light I heard scrambling noises below and ran down and turned on another light and saw this man going out through the basement window and my Gwendolen pulling on her clothes. I tried to grab her arms and was yelling at her, and she pulled one arm loose and clawed at my face and kneed me in the groin. I twisted her arm, and she turned her back and kept trying to kick my shins, and I got my arm around her neck and jerked her off the floor and, oh God, I don't know—it was a nightmare. When she went limp and I let her down and tried to revive her, she never made a sound or showed a sign of life."

He lowered his head and his body shuddered convulsively, but he made no sound.

"Did you go through her room that night?"

He took a deep breath, straightened up slightly, and nodded.

"There wasn't a lot, but there was enough. He had written to her, and she had put her thoughts and dreams into her diaries.

He had completely seduced her mind, and they had met at least once before. She was completely out of her mind over him."

He raised his head and stared across the athletic field.

"He told her she was the most intelligent girl he'd ever met, that she would be a poet, that she was beautiful and the essence of everything a man could dream of. He told her exactly what she wanted to hear, far beyond what her teachers or that Bible school man could ever offer. Everything she had always wanted to hear, all her life. He promised to take her to California and marry her."

I kept still, and after a few moments he glanced at me.

"When I read those things he said, and saw the way she reacted, I couldn't hate him anymore. And when I couldn't hate him, the horror of what I'd done buried me. I just wanted to die."

"And then you learned a little bit about other women in Derek's life."

"Yes. At first I fought against it, but then it was almost a liberation, and finally it became a cause. I could almost convince myself I had saved Gwendolen from inevitable heartbreak and misery, which would have come with her disillusionment."

"Who told you about him first, Purita?"

"Yes. Right after Gwendolen died. She told me about Derek and what he had done to her, and told me what she thought he had done to Gwendolen."

"Why didn't she tell Driscoll?"

"She doesn't like or trust him. She's convinced he'd only assume she was after revenge and would consider her a bitter woman with a grudge and not truly a victim."

"Did she offer to help you get him for killing your daughter?"

"It was never that open, no. But I know she would have. She'd never let me be punished for killing him."

"Did you tell her you had?"

His head drooped again.

"Yes. I've never been able to lie to her."

"How long have you been lovers?"

"Only since Gwendolen's death. The week after. She was so understanding, so forgiving—"

"You told her after the first time?"

"Before. I couldn't have her without telling her the truth."

We sat in silence for a few minutes and watched as a couple kids in their early teens went out on the nearest playing field and started playing catch with a scruffy baseball.

"Doc," I said, "did Derek try to blackmail you?"

He took a deep breath, and nodded.

"What was his approach?"

"He said he had waited outside the church after sneaking out the window, expecting to see Gwendolen and me come out—but only I showed up. He went back through the window and found her dead and, guessing that he'd be accused, got out and left town. But when he got thinking about it, he decided he could scare me into paying for his silence, and he telephoned me at my office, told me what he knew, and said if I gave him enough money, he would leave the territory and everyone would assume he'd been the killer, and I'd be safe."

"Did you agree to pay?"

"I told him I would, but it would take some time, since I didn't have the kind of money he demanded."

"How much?"

"Ten thousand dollars."

"How were you to pay him?"

"I'd send the money to a post office box in Sioux Falls."

"You found out he was staying in that farmhouse from the anonymous letters, right?"

"Yes."

I asked if he would be willing to go see Driscoll with me.

"No. I'll get a lawyer and then see him. And I'll tell you now, I'll confess to killing Warford, but will never admit to anything beyond that. Do you understand? I killed him for what he did to my daughter, and that is all I'll admit."

"No argument. Who'll your lawyer be?"

"Wes Nelson, from Corden. Perhaps you know him."

"Oh yeah. He'll probably like the job. So I'll see you tomorrow?"

"As soon as I can work things out."

We left it at that.

37

I think the toughest thing for Doc Westcott was when Purita quietly left town. Nobody told me if there had been an understanding between them, but it made sense that she figured his chances of getting off easy would be about 95 percent improved if his marriage wasn't split up in the midst of the trial. From the general reactions around town in the week I spent there after Doc turned himself in, it seemed his killing of Derek would, if anything, improve his practice, but Hazel told me if he abandoned his wife, it would be another matter completely. In fact, if much got around about his involvement with Purita, it might have a bad effect on the trial and the sort of sentence the doctor would face.

So practicalities took over, and as usual, romance went down the tubes.

Well, not for me. Hazel picked our wedding date for late September, Ma accepted the job of hosting, and of course Bertha would bear the weight of it and be proud.